Her pulse spiked as his fingers entangled in her hair.

How could she possibly react to his touch this way when her very life was in a state of chaotic danger? Nonetheless, desire grew red-hot inside her. She stretched out beside Dylan, spread her hand over the bare hardness of his chest and pressed her lips against his.

He kissed her back, tentatively at first, but then ravenously, as if he couldn't get enough. She trembled in his arms as the hot, deep, slow, kisses awakened a throbbing passion inside her.

She knew if they didn't stop soon, they wouldn't stop at all. Did she care?

Her question was disrupted by the tones of Dylan's cell phone.

The delicious moment faded into oblivion as she watched his expression turn grim. Cold chills replaced the warmth in her veins and reality returned with a punishing vengeance.

JOANNA WAYNE

COWBOY SWAGGER

HARLEQUIN®

TORONTO • NEW YORK • LONDON
AMSTERDAM • PARIS • SYDNEY • HAMBURG
STOCKHOLM • ATHENS • TOKYO • MILAN • MADRID
PRAGUE • WARSAW • BUDAPEST • AUCKLAND

To all my readers who love cowboys.
To my grandsons who have taught me
what it means to totally lose your heart to a child—
though they are growing up fast. And to my hubby
who will spend many hours driving me around the
beautiful Texas Hill Country to research the setting
for the books in the Sons of Troy Ledger.

ISBN-13: 978-0-373-74549-4

COWBOY SWAGGER

Copyright © 2010 by Jo Ann Vest

Recycling programs
for this product may
not exist in your area.

ABOUT THE AUTHOR

Joanna Wayne was born and raised in Shreveport, Louisiana, and received her undergraduate and graduate degrees from LSU-Shreveport. She moved to New Orleans in 1984, and it was there that she attended her first writing class and joined her first professional writing organization. Her debut novel, *Deep in the Bayou*, was published in 1994.

Now, dozens of published books later, Joanna has made a name for herself as being on the cutting edge of romantic suspense in both series and single-title novels. She has been on the Waldenbooks bestseller list for romance and has won many industry awards. She is also a popular speaker at writing organizations and local community functions and has taught creative writing at the University of New Orleans Metropolitan College.

Joanna currently resides in a small community forty miles north of Houston, Texas, with her husband. Though she still has many family and emotional ties to Louisiana, she loves living in the Lone Star state. You may write Joanna at P.O. Box 265, Montgomery, Texas 77356.

Books by Joanna Wayne

CAST OF CHARACTERS

Dylan Ledger—Troy Ledger's son. He needs to settle a few things with the father he hasn't seen or talked to since the conviction.

Collette McGuire—The feisty daughter of the town sheriff is being stalked by a madman.

Troy Ledger—Convicted seventeen years ago for the murder of his wife and released on a technicality.

Helene Ledger—Troy's wife/Dylan's mother who was brutally murdered when Dylan was only eleven years old.

Sheriff Glenn McGuire—Tough on crime and on anyone who gets in his way.

Mildred McGuire—Collette's mother.

Abby—She owns the local diner and is famous for her pies—and her gossip.

Eleanor Baker—A friend of Collette's known for her in-depth investigative reporting.

Melissa Kingston—Friend of Collette's. Owns and edits a new paranormal magazine with Eleanor.

Bill and Alma McGuire—Collette's brother and his wife.

Georgia McGuire—Collette's niece.

Sukey—Housekeeper.

Able Drake—Old friend of Troy's who's willing to help in any way he can.

Bob Adkins—Well-respected citizen of Mustang Run who lends Troy horses; one of the few who stand by Troy.

Wyatt Ledger—Dylan's older brother, a detective.

Ruthanne—A good friend of Helene Ledger who seems to want back in Troy's life.

Chapter One

Murderer's kid! Murderer's kid! Murderer's kid!

The taunts reverberated inside Dylan Ledger's brain as he approached the Mustang Run Elementary School. Seventeen years after his father's conviction, distant echoes of the mocking still tied knots in his stomach.

Or maybe it was the significance of the day that brought the old rancor home to roost. His father's homecoming. The murderer's return to the scene of the crime, as one radio news announcer had so bluntly put it.

Dylan slowed and stared out the window of his truck. The flagpole was topped with the American colors, and just below that the Lone Star State banner waved in the gentle breeze. Cows grazed the fence line that kept them off the playground.

Kids were filing out of the building to board the yellow school buses that had lined up in front of the building. It was late May, but apparently classes were still in session.

Cars formed another line, mothers waiting to take their children home. Memories flooded his mind. He and his brothers had waited in that line on the fatal day eighteen years ago this September. His mother had never come.

He grimaced and pushed the memories back to the dark crevices of his mind, the way he'd learned to do years ago.

Only now that he was back in the town where his life had been ripped apart, he realized he wasn't nearly as detached from the past horrors as he'd thought. Even worse, he wasn't sure why he'd come back or what he really hoped to gain from this.

The traffic light in front of the school turned red. His gaze drifted to a woman who'd just stepped from her vehicle and was waving frantically, probably trying to get the attention of her kid. The woman's hair was so red it looked like fire in the bright sunlight.

She turned his way for a second. His gaze was riveted on her, not only because she was a knockout. She reminded him of someone, though he had no idea whom.

The light turned green. He lowered the truck's window as he drove slowly through the town and then turned onto the narrow dirt road that led to the family ranch. The odors of earth, grass and even the occasional whiff of manure were a welcome change from the smells of car exhaust and fish from the open market a few steps from his tiny apartment back in Boston.

Rolling hills stretched in all directions as far as he could see. A grouping of magnificent horses stood in a fenced pasture, mingling with a few young colts. A cluster of persimmon trees gave shade to some longhorns. A dog barked in the distance, and a flock of coal-black crows cawed noisily from their perch atop a weathered gate. In a few miles he'd be home.

Who was he kidding? He had no real home. Not in Texas and certainly not back in Boston where he'd never really fit in.

A tractor bounced and rumbled along the road in front of him. Dylan slowed. The driver of the tractor pulled to the edge of the road and gave a two-fingered wave as Dylan passed him.

A minute or two later, a red Jeep Wrangler bore down on him from behind, passing the tractor and riding the tail of Dylan's truck for a minute before passing him, as well. The driver of the vehicle appeared to have a cell phone glued to her ear. He couldn't be sure due to the mass of wild, red curls that tumbled to her shoulders.

Same hair. Same vehicle. It had to be the woman who'd captured his attention at the school, but there was no child in the Jeep. Her car disappeared around the next curve. She was in a damn big hurry to get somewhere.

Another vehicle came up behind him, chased Dylan's bumper around a curve and then passed him. The van had the name of an Austin TV channel emblazoned on the door. It hit Dylan then that they were rushing to the same place he was heading. The media were once again gathering at the Ledger ranch with teeth bared.

Fury burned in Dylan's veins as he drove the rest of the way. Did the media never have the decency to just back off?

The metal gate was propped open. The wheels of his truck rattled over the cattle gap, and he kept driving. There was no need to latch the hook; the varmints were already inside.

A sense of gruesome déjà vu attacked him as he drove the quarter of a mile to the house. But he wasn't a kid any longer. He'd handle whatever came his way.

COLLETTE MCGUIRE GAVE UP on finding a decent parking spot and left her Jeep in a grassy area just north of the house. She grabbed her camera, then pushed through the dozen or so reporters and photographers who were clumped around the front door of the Ledger ranch house.

A lot like vultures, she thought, guilt surfacing that she was one of them.

She shivered and looked around her, always wary, hating the unfamiliar fear that had crawled inside her over the past few weeks.

"There you are. I've been looking all over for you."

She turned to find her friend, Eleanor Baker, maneuvering through the restless reporters and heading her way.

"Thanks for answering my SOS," Eleanor said.

"Next time could you give me a little more notice? I had already told Alma I'd pick up Georgia from school on my way home and take her shopping. Her eleventh birthday is this weekend."

"Your niece is already eleven?"

"Yes. Can you believe it?"

"Not really." Eleanor glanced around. "Where is she?"

"I got to the school in time to have her catch the bus. I postponed the shopping trip."

"You can take her when we're through."

"There won't be time. I'm working a wedding tonight. Georgia is not happy. Both you and Melinda owe me big-time."

"Get me some great shots of Troy Ledger arriving at the little house of horrors and we'll both be in your debt."

"So the infamous Mr. Ledger hasn't arrived yet?"

"No sign of him, but according to reports of when he left the prison, he could drive up any minute."

"What happened to Melinda?"

"She's on assignment in Austin for her real boss. You know, the guy who actually pays her. She thought she'd be back in time to help me out, but got stuck in traffic."

"So that's why I got drafted."

"Which reminds me, do you mind if I camp out at your place tonight? I have an interview scheduled with a developer just outside Mustang Run at an ungodly hour in the morning."

"You want my house *and* my expertise with the camera? That will cost you," Collette teased.

"Let's hope this turns out to be worth it."

"Take the left side of my garage tonight. I'll park on the right."

"I remember. You know, you may actually be better at this assignment than Melinda."

"Not likely. Ghosts are not within my area of expertise," said Collette.

"No, but you're local. That should be worth something. Pictures of Troy Ledger inside the haunted house would catapult *Beyond the Grave* to the hottest paranormal magazine on the racks. And then I could actually pay Melinda—and myself."

"Local or not, fat chance I'll get inside that house. I'll be lucky if I get a shot of him entering the door."

"Then I guess Melinda and I will be forced to break in the house the first time Troy Ledger leaves."

Collette covered her ears. "Don't confess planned illegalities to me. I'm the sheriff's daughter."

"Like you'd turn us in to him. You barely speak to the man."

"Yes, and let's keep it that way."

"Speaking of illegalities, are you still getting calls from that weirdo?"

"Occasionally. The calls are pretty lame, but they're starting to get to me."

"Sic the sheriff on him."

"I don't know what he could do since the guy only spouts harmless utterances of devotion. What are you hoping to get today for the article?" Collette asked, changing the subject.

"I'm thinking the tag will be 'Troy Ledger returns to the house that drove him to murder,'" Eleanor said, holding up her hands as if framing the article.

"Last I heard, he was still claiming his

innocence. And he was released from prison." Collette removed her camera from the case and adjusted the lens.

"Sure, but released on a technicality," Eleanor countered.

"The prison psychiatrist interviewed on the morning news claimed Troy Ledger has never shown one sign of violent behavior since his conviction. She said she's certain of his mental stability and even went so far as to say that she wouldn't hesitate to trust him with her own son."

"Shrinks, what do they know?" Eleanor glanced at her watch. "Do you think he killed his wife?"

"My opinion doesn't count for much. I was ten at the time."

"Your dad must think he's guilty. He arrested him." Eleanor stretched for a better look as a commotion ensued at the back of the crowd.

A black pickup truck approached, driving up to the front door and sending the reporters who'd gathered there flying to get out of the way. A sexy hunk of a man in boots, worn jeans and a Western hat climbed out, a man who was decades too young to be Troy Ledger.

He looked around and shook his head before stamping to the door. Once there, he pulled a ring of keys from his pocket and poked one into the lock.

"Holy Smoley," Eleanor said lustfully. "I'd sleep with ghosts any night as long as that cowboy was in the bed with us. Do you know him?"

"He could be one of Troy Ledger's sons. I think he had four."

"Five," Eleanor corrected. "Dakota, Tyler, Dylan, Sean and Wyatt."

"You've done your homework."

"And a couple of major investigative articles on the crime. FYI, I think Troy Ledger is as guilty as sin and I renege on any offer to sleep with one of his sons, not even if it guaranteed me a picture of ghosts."

Collette aimed and started shooting, still looking for something familiar to help her identify the stranger. She'd known a few of Troy Ledger's sons, but that was years ago when they were mere boys.

The guy pushed open the door but didn't go inside. Instead he scanned the crowd as if looking for someone. Flashbulbs popped, and he blinked and squinted in defense. Reporters started yelling questions and trying to stick mikes in his face.

"Are you a relative of Troy Ledger?"

"Is Troy coming back to the ranch?"

"Will he move back to Mustang Run?"

The cowboy put up a hand as if to quiet the

group. Amazingly, they obliged him, though Collette was certain the cooperation wouldn't last long unless he gave them something they wanted.

"You're trespassing," he said. "And looking for a story that was milked dry seventeen years ago."

"Who are you?" a reporter yelled from the back of the group.

"Dylan Ledger, son of the convicted murderer." He tipped his hat as if mocking them and propped a hand on the door frame.

Dylan. She remembered him more than the others. He had been a year ahead of her and had ridden the same bus to school and back. Even then he'd been cute, but he'd aged to perfection.

Someone pushed a mike into his face. "Have you forgiven your father for killing your mother?"

"My relationship with my father is none of your business."

"Is your father going to live here on Willow Creek Ranch?"

"I have no idea what my father's plans are for the future. End of story, so you may as well go out and find yourselves some real news."

He scanned the crowd again. When his gaze fixed, Collette was certain that he was looking right at her. She felt the impact of his stare right down to her toes, a kind of heated awareness that set her on edge.

Eleanor poked her in the ribs with her elbow. "He recognizes you."

"No way. I was scrawny and wore braces when he saw me last."

"And now you're gorgeous and you've acquired breasts. You've got his attention. Ask him a question."

"I'm a photographer, not a reporter."

"He doesn't know that." She took Collette's free hand and waved it in the air. "Ask him if he thinks the house is haunted."

Again, Dylan stared straight at Collette. "I'll grant one interview," he conceded, as if it were an afterthought. "In private. The redhead in the jeans and yellow shirt," he said, pointing at Collette.

Eleanor slapped her on the back and pushed her forward. "Go get 'em, girl. But don't forget the pictures. And be careful."

Collette panicked. She didn't represent a legitimate news organization, and she'd never conducted a real interview. She was terrific at what she did, but that was photography, usually for weddings or at least happy family occasions.

Eleanor gave her another shove. "What are you waiting on?"

Collette gave up and pushed her way through

the crowd. Some reporters moved out of her way to make it easier for her. A few guys deliberately blocked her path, and two made sexist comments about her looks doing her work for her.

She had a couple of words for them, too, but she managed enough restraint to keep them to herself. When she reached Dylan, he escorted her inside and closed and locked the door behind them. Her stomach rolled, though she couldn't blame the uneasiness on the house's aura. It looked and felt like any other sprawling ranch house, except for the musty odors that came from years of being closed off from life, wind and sun.

Dylan's hand brushed the back of a worn leather couch as he walked past it. "At least the air conditioner works."

And worked well, she noted. The house was pleasantly cool and free of dust and the myriad spiderwebs that would have given it a true haunted look. Someone had obviously readied the place for Troy Ledger's arrival.

Dylan walked to the kitchen. She followed him.

He opened what appeared to be a new refrigerator. "There are soft drinks, bottled water and beer," he said. "What's your pleasure?"

"Water would be nice."

He handed her a bottle of water and took a beer for himself. She nodded her thanks.

He unscrewed the top from his beer. The silence grew awkward.

"Why me?" she finally asked.

"You passed me back on the road."

"That's not much of a reason."

He took a long swig of the beer. "Guess I just wanted to know why the hurry. Is news that scarce in Mustang Run?"

"Frankly, yes."

"Must be an exciting town."

"About the same as when we were at Mustang Run Elementary School."

His eyes narrowed. "Should I recognize you?"

"I'd worry if you did. I've changed a lot since fifth grade. I'm Collette McGuire. I was a year behind you in school."

He nodded as if he'd just had an ah-ha moment. "Collette the tattletale. You're right. You've definitely changed. Is your father still sheriff?"

Her only claim to fame. In this case, it would work against her. "Yes, he is."

"Is he part of the welcoming committee waiting outside?"

"I didn't see him out there. As far as I can tell, the mob is all media sharks."

"Like you?"

"Not exactly. I mean I am with the media today, but I'm not a reporter."

His eyebrows arched.

"I'm a photographer—with *Beyond the Grave*," she added hesitantly. "It's a magazine that explores the paranormal."

His muscles bunched, and his lips pulled into a tight line. "Let me guess. You want to help me connect with my dead mother."

Ire burned in her veins. "I don't communicate with the dead." Or some of the living, either, she silently added.

He took another swig of the beer and leaned against the counter. "So why is *Beyond the Grave* interested in Willow Creek Ranch?"

"Word around town is that your house is haunted."

"You people need to get a life."

In theory she agreed with him. That didn't keep his arrogance from rubbing her the wrong way. He'd been gone for years. What did he know of their town or her? But she should probably cut him some slack considering the reason he'd come back to Mustang Run. Besides, Eleanor and Melinda did need those pictures.

She placed her camera case on the kitchen table. "I realize the timing is not the greatest for you, but since you invited me inside, why not let me take a few pictures? And if there's anything you want to say for the magazine, I can see that you're quoted accurately."

"I've nothing to say. But go ahead. Take your pictures." He glanced at his watch. "Make it fast. My father will be here any minute now, and I seriously doubt he'll be as accommodating as I'm being."

"Thanks for the warning." She started snapping pictures of the kitchen. Try as she might, she couldn't find a way to make the place look spooky. She fared no better in the family room. The space just looked lonesome and bereft of human touch.

Intent on working quickly, she didn't notice that Dylan had joined her in the family room until she caught sight of him in her viewfinder.

Her heart skipped a beat or two from the sheer masculinity of the man against the backdrop of the huge stone fireplace. The slow burn he ignited crept to her cheeks. She lowered the camera without taking the shot.

Dylan propped a booted foot on the low hearth and an elbow on the mantel. "What makes people say the house is haunted?"

"Some claim that they've seen a woman in white out by the gate when they pass it at night. She tries to wave them down as if she needs help. If they stop, she disappears."

"Is that it?"

"Not quite. Some claim to have seen a woman standing at one of the windows."

"Superstitious fools." Dylan raked his fingers through his hair, parting the sandy locks into deep grooves that quickly filled back in place. "Are you one of them?"

"One of the superstitious fools? No. I have too much trouble with the living to worry about ghosts."

Her cell phone rang. Probably Eleanor with instructions as to what photos she wanted for the magazine. "Excuse me," she said, reaching for her phone.

"No problem."

"Hello."

"I saw you go inside the house with Dylan Ledger."

Apprehension ground in her stomach. The lunatic who'd been stalking her must have followed her to Willow Creek Ranch.

She walked back to the kitchen, hopefully out of Dylan's hearing range. "I told you to stop calling me," she whispered.

"I can't do that. We're soul mates, Collette, meant to be together."

She took a deep breath, hoping it would settle her shaky nerves and shakier voice. "I'm not anything to you, and if you don't stop harassing me, my father will arrest you, throw you in jail and lose the key."

"I'm not afraid of your daddy, Collette. But I have a message for him. Tell him I'll soon be sleeping with his precious daughter. And you'll like it. I promise you that."

Her skin crawled. As much as she dreaded the thought, she was going to have to get a gun. This guy was nuts.

She broke the connection and rejoined Dylan. "I'm sorry for the interruption."

"You look upset. Is something wrong?"

"It was a nuisance call." She tried to take another picture, but her hands shook and she had trouble holding the camera steady.

"Are you sure you're okay?" Dylan asked.

He was far too astute to buy her feeble excuses. "Yeah, I'm okay. It's just that there's this guy who's bothering me. I'll deal with it."

She went back to taking pictures, and this time her hands remained calm. She finished in record time and walked to the kitchen. Dylan was staring out the window, his face a hard mask that revealed no emotion. She felt a weird connection with him, as if growing up in Mustang Run were a bond in itself.

She stepped closer. "It must be tough coming back after all these years. It's a nice thing to do for your father."

He shook his head. "I'm not sure I'm doing it for him."

So things weren't fully settled between them, which made his inviting her in even more strange. "Did you stay in touch with him over the years?"

He shrugged. "Does it matter?"

Which meant he considered it none of her business. Fair enough. Only he was the one who'd started with the questions. "Why did you really let me in to take the pictures, Dylan?"

"You looked familiar. I just realized it's because you look like your mother."

"You remember my mother? I wasn't even aware that you'd met her."

"She came over the day my mother was murdered. She cooked dinner for my brothers and me. My memories from that night are sketchy, but I remember her telling us that no one would hurt us and that it was all right to cry. She stayed until my grandparents got here."

"Where was your dad?"

"Being questioned by the deputies—and your father."

Yep, that pretty much defined her parents. Mom had always been there to comfort. Her dad was always there to find fault and uncover the hidden sins.

"How is your mother?" Dylan asked.

"She had a stroke and passed away a few years ago."

"I'm sorry, "Dylan said. "Go ahead with your pictures. My father won't like it, but the skeletons have been rattling around in this house for too long already. Might as well shake a few out for your readers."

His voice was gruff and his tone edgy, an attempt, she suspected, to hide his emotions. Dylan was all man in every way that showed, but somewhere deep inside him, there must be some remnant of the boy who lost not only his mother to a brutal murder, but life as he knew it.

The clatter of voices outside rose to a crescendo. She joined Dylan at the window. A white truck was speeding down the road to the house.

"The return of Troy Ledger," Dylan said.

Troy Ledger, not his father. That said a lot. His father might have gotten a get-out-of-jail-free card, but he obviously wasn't getting a pass from Dylan. Maybe she had more in common with Dylan than she'd thought.

Surprising herself, she pulled out a business card. "If you need to talk, I'm available. You can call my photography studio or my cell number. Or you can stop by anytime. I live in the old Callister place. It's the yellow house just past the Baptist church."

"Your husband might not appreciate that."

"What makes you think I'm married?"

"I saw you at the elementary school when I passed."

"I was there to pick up my brother's daughter, or rather to tell her I couldn't pick her up and that she should ride the bus home."

Their eyes met again as he took the card from her. His were tempestuous, yet mysteriously seductive. "I hope this works out for you," she said.

"Yeah. Same for you. Be careful with the jerk who's giving you a hard time." He handed her the camera case and then walked her to the front door just as the back door swung open. "See you around."

"Yeah, cowboy. See you around."

She had a feeling he wouldn't be looking her up. That was probably for the best, she told herself. He was far too complicated. She'd seen that in his intense, brandy-colored eyes. And she had complications and problems enough of her own.

Oddly, though, she found herself hoping that he'd call.

Chapter Two

He kept his distance, remaining unnoticed from his position behind the woodshed and sheltered by the low branches of a spreading live oak tree. Lifting his binoculars to his eyes, he watched as Collette McGuire walked out of the house and squeezed through the mob of reporters who were all but wetting their pants over the arrival of what looked to be the infamous Troy Ledger.

The wind tousled her hair like a lover might, lifting and teasing the fiery red curls before letting them fall to her narrow shoulders. Collette McGuire was both beautiful and spunky. Neither altered the outcome, but they had changed the game, likely even prolonged it.

She was a woman who could tempt any red-blooded male, even one as scarred and damaged as he was.

Too bad she had to die.

Chapter Three

Dylan dried the plate and put it away. The dishes were old, probably the same ones they'd eaten off of when he was a kid. Still, they were as unfamiliar to him as the man standing next to him.

Troy Ledger was tall and gaunt with slight bags under his tortured eyes and wrinkles that dug deep furrows across his brow. His nails were chewed down to his flesh, and a jagged scar ran along his right cheek and down to his breastbone. His forearms were muscled. He'd likely be a tough contender in a fight.

Fifty-five years old but he looked like a man who'd lived through hell. He acted only half alive, as if he'd been reduced to going through the motions, except that twice that afternoon he'd seemed to be in the grip of a mood so intense he could barely control it. One of those times, he'd clutched the glass he was holding so tightly that it shattered in his hand.

Dylan would have liked to ask what he was

thinking at that moment, but his dad had set the rules of engagement from the moment he'd walked into the house. They'd shared a quick handshake and greeting, and then his dad had withdrawn so deeply into himself, Dylan might as well have been invisible.

They'd spoken briefly since then—about the steaks Dylan had grilled for their dinner, about the price of beef these days, about the weather. The closest they'd come to anything personal was when the formidable Troy Ledger had asked Dylan if he was married. He'd said no. His dad had only nodded. Who in hell knew what that meant?

His brothers had been right. Coming here was a mistake. But now that he was here, he'd stick it out at least a few more days. No reason to hurry off. No one was waiting for him anywhere.

"What are you going to do about the ranch?" Dylan asked when the dishes were all put away.

"Raise cattle, same as other ranchers."

"Cattle cost money."

He was pretty sure his dad didn't have any. They were never rich, and the little Troy would have been swallowed up by lawyers' fees and taxes on the ranch.

Dylan had learned that much from his father's attorney who'd handled the estate—the estate consisting of the ranch and this old house. The attorney had contacted Dylan and his brothers when their father's release had become imminent and suggested they welcome him home. Dylan had been the only one who'd accepted the proposal. At his father's request, the attorney had mailed Dylan a key to the house.

The family of Dylan's mother was in much better financial shape. His and his brothers' inheritance from their grandparents had gone into a trust fund that had put them all through college.

Uncle Phil had been upset when Dylan decided to go into the army after graduation instead of joining his uncle's extremely successful advertising firm. Dylan had wanted to do something for his country and he'd needed adventure. The army had offered both.

Troy stuffed his hands in the back pockets of his jeans. "Able Drake's backing me for a start-up herd."

"Do I know him?"

"Not likely. Lives up in Dallas now, but he's from these parts."

Dylan couldn't help but wonder if Able was someone Troy had met in prison. As far as he knew, no one on his mother's side of the family had ever mentioned the man, but then they hadn't even spoken his father's name in years. They were all convinced he'd killed their beloved Helene.

Dylan had acted as if he believed it, too. But he hadn't. The father who lived in his dreams and imagination could never have killed his mother.

"Is Able the one who readied the house for you?" Dylan asked.

"He had it done." His father looked around as if noticing the place for the first time. "Not much of a house, is it?"

"Structure's okay," Dylan said. It was the only positive thing he could think of.

"Used to look better," his dad said. "Back when…" He stopped midsentence, looking as if pain was digging into his ruddy flesh like sharp nails.

"Yeah," Dylan agreed. "It used to be better."

His dad rubbed the old scar. "I'm beat. Think I'll head on off to bed."

And avoid any more feeble attempts at conversation with the son he hadn't seen since the day he'd been convicted. All the boys had been there that day to say goodbye, against their grandparents' will.

Dylan tried to muster up a bit of resentment for his father's eagerness to escape his company. It didn't come. Truth was, he wasn't up to talking tonight, either. The chasm that separated them after years of zero communication was too deep and wide to be bridged by a steak and a few attempts at meaningless small talk.

"I'll take the back bedroom," his dad said.

Not the big bedroom he'd shared with Dylan's mom, though Dylan had spotted him standing at that door earlier, staring into the room, his muscles strained and his expression as pained as if he'd been kicked in the gut by an angry bull.

Dylan sure as hell wasn't sleeping there, either. "I'll take my old bedroom. I checked earlier and it looks like all the beds have new sheets on them."

"Guess the old ones would have rotted by now."

Troy walked away, leaving Dylan standing alone in the kitchen. Memories gathered around him like a suffocating fog. His mom stirring big pots of stews and soups at the range. Her singing while she worked. Trays of fresh-baked cookies cooling on the counter. Her long hair flying when she'd grab him and dance about the kitchen. Her fragrance when she'd pull him into a hug. Her arms around him when he'd had a nightmare.

Returning footfalls in the hallway yanked him from the bittersweet reveries. He swallowed hard and turned to see his dad's tall, lean body filling the open doorway.

"Thanks for being here, Dylan."

The words were husky, as if they'd been pushed

through a scratchy throat. His dad's eyes looked moist. Dylan's started to burn.

"Sure thing," Dylan said. "We'll talk more tomorrow."

"Yeah. Tomorrow."

He turned away as his dad's retreating footsteps echoed down the hallway. The connection had been brief, but it had been there. It was a start.

Dylan searched the cupboard for a real drink, something strong enough to fight off the memories and regrets. He found a bottle of whiskey. Not his brand but now was not the time to be choosy.

He poured a couple of fingers of the amber liquid into a glass, swirled it around and then sipped it, welcoming the burn that trailed down his dry throat. He pushed through the back door and into the gray of twilight. Too restless to sit, he finished the drink, left the glass on the back steps and walked to his truck.

He'd be back, but right now he had to get out of here before the ghosts from his past made the woman in white who appeared for the superstitious think she was living in a freakin' mausoleum.

COLLETTE RAISED THE CAMERA and framed the image of the bride dancing with her preadolescent nephew, an adorable red-haired lad who was stepping all over the hem of her gorgeous gown. The bride, Isabelle Smith, barely twenty-one herself, showed no sign of irritation.

This was her day, and the glow of love emanated from her like stardust. The only bad thing about stardust was that it had such a limited shelf life.

Not that Collette had anything against marriage. She might even take the plunge one day—just not any day soon. She liked her independence and had never met a man who'd tempted her to become a "we" instead of a "me." But she had to admit, the bride did look ravishing and blissfully in love.

Collette had known Isabelle and her whole family for years. They went to the same church that Collette had grown up in, and Isabelle's father had helped Collette raise a prize-winning pig back in her 4-H days. Her own father had been too busy enforcing the law and making inane rules for her and her mother to follow.

She also knew the groom and his family. Carl Knight's dad owned the local hardware and feed store. His mother taught at the new consolidated high school. Carl was in the Marines and had worn full-dress uniform for the ceremony. He'd be shipping off for Afghanistan soon.

Even as she'd taken pictures of the couple

exchanging the vows, Collette had prayed he'd return safely. She suspected many of the guests were doing the same.

She moved to another corner of the dance floor that had been set up beneath the white tent. The country band switched from a lively two-step to a romantic ballad, and Isabelle's grandparents joined the group on the dance floor. Collette couldn't help but smile as she got a couple of great shots of them snuggled in each other's arms and swaying to the music.

Setting her camera on a nearby table, she checked her watch. The reception would start winding down soon, but she was sure that she had enough formal and candid shots to satisfy the bride and her family. At least she would once she captured the newlyweds leaving for their honeymoon.

"Care to dance?"

She spun around at the unfamiliar voice.

"Sorry. I didn't mean to startle you."

"You didn't," she lied. "I just didn't know anyone was behind me." Stupid response considering they were beneath a rather crowded tent. She hated that the recent phone calls had made her so apprehensive that she sometimes jumped at her own shadow.

"I'm Brady Collins, friend of the groom."

He extended his hand. A nice hand, she had to

admit, attached to a slim blond guy with cobalt-blue eyes and an enticing smile. There was no spark when his hand wrapped around hers. Obviously, he was no Dylan Ledger.

"I'm Collette McGuire, the photographer."

"I noticed. You've been doing a heck of a job, but I'm sure the happy couple would forgive your abandoning your post for one dance."

"The offer is tempting, but not in my contract."

"Ah, the prettiest woman at the reception would have to be a woman of principle."

"Thanks," she said, "though we both know the prettiest woman at the wedding tonight is unquestionably Isabelle."

"Only because she has the unfair advantage of the wedding glow."

Carl picked that moment to rescue his bride from the awkwardly energetic nephew. Collette reached for her camera. "Your friend Carl looks pretty happy himself. Now, if you'll excuse me, I really do have to get back to work."

"Can't blame a guy for asking."

She didn't, but even if she hadn't been working, she wasn't really interested in meeting anyone tonight. Working the wedding had helped, but the stalker's call this afternoon had left her more nervous than usual. Not only that, but try as she might, she hadn't been able to fully shake Dylan from her mind.

She doubted he'd call, but instead of turning her cell phone off completely as she usually did when working an affair, she'd left it on vibrate tonight. There was no rational explanation for how he'd affected her. All she knew was that she wanted to see and talk to him again.

She took a few more pictures and then stepped outside the tent, walking a few yards away for a breath of fresh air. Silvery strings of moonlight filtered through the trees, and the music that had been loud and vibrating inside the tent was softly romantic in the background.

She took out her phone and called her house, not that she had any doubts Eleanor had made herself at home once Collette had left for the wedding. Eleanor was outgoing and resourceful, no doubt part of the reason for her success as a freelance investigative reporter. And they had been friends since their first year at the University of Texas.

The phone rang until the answering machine picked up. Disappointment swelled. Eleanor must have decided to drive back to Austin instead of spending the night after all.

Ordinarily, Collette was fine going home at night to an empty house. Her stalker had infiltrated those feelings of safety, replacing them with irritating spurts of apprehension. If the calls kept up, she was going to have to break down and buy a gun or maybe get a dog. A big, ferocious-looking dog who'd bark like crazy if anyone came sneaking around the house she rented from the Callisters. Maybe she'd get both.

Mustang Run was a peaceful town, but it hadn't totally escaped violence. She'd been reminded of that quite vividly while taking pictures inside the Ledger home today.

She wondered if a dog or a gun would have saved Dylan's mother. Not likely if Troy Ledger was actually guilty of killing her.

Thoughts of Dylan crowded into Collette's mind. She did her best to push them aside. She didn't need a guy with a tortured soul in her life. But impulsively she slipped her hand into her pocket and let it slide across the leather case that held her cell phone.

The phone remained still and silent.

DYLAN TIPPED THE BOTTLE of cold beer to his lips and took a long swig. Mack's Haven was exactly how he would have pictured a typical small-town Texas bar. Smoky. Loud. Friendly. A down-home kind of place. A worn wooden sign pronounced, "No Dancing on the bar with your spurs on."

Smoky and loud didn't bother Dylan. Nor did

the sign, since he not only didn't own a pair of spurs, he had no plans for dancing on the bar. Neither was anyone else at the present time, though the cozy dance floor was crowded.

The friendly part of the equation was the drawback. Far too many of the patrons had felt it their duty to introduce themselves and make the stranger welcome.

Dylan probably came across as antisocial, but explaining who he was would have led to questions he couldn't answer about his return to Mustang Run. So far he'd managed to give only a first name and resist the invitations to dance by a couple of affable young women. Another beer and he might not be so inclined.

He hadn't planned to end up here tonight, but when the musky memories from the day his mother had been killed began to pound inside his skull, he'd spotted the bar and seen it as a temporary escape.

The buxom blonde waitress in a seductive cotton T-shirt and a pair of denim shorts returned to his table. "Want another of the same?"

"Better not." He pulled out his wallet. "What do I owe you?"

"Two beers—ten dollars and eighty cents."

He gave her a ten and a five.

"Thanks." She took the money but didn't walk away as he stood to leave.

"Are you new to the area or just passing through?"

"Most likely passing through. You take care," he said and walked away before she followed up with another question.

He climbed in his truck, revved the engine and started back to the ranch, slowing as he passed the house he'd already identified as the one in which Collette McGuire lived. Lights were on. She was still up, though not necessarily alone.

Still, she had said stop by anytime.

He pulled in the driveway and kept his truck running. There was no sign of Collette's Jeep, but she could have parked it in the garage.

He wondered what the hell he was thinking driving up to somebody's house this time of the night. Not to mention that he'd be opening himself up to a barrage of intrusive questions.

He should turn the truck around right now before Collette spotted him. But the dread of going back to the ranch tonight got all mixed up with the crazy desire to see Collette again. She'd been easy to talk to, almost like running into an old friend in the midst of an enemy camp.

He shut off the car and, just as he killed the lights, he caught a glimpse of movement behind the house. It could have been a large dog or possibly a deer, but it had sure looked like a person. He turned the headlights on again, but whatever it was had disappeared into the trees and shadows.

An owl hooted in the distance as he got out of the truck and walked the uneven concrete path to the steps. Light from inside the house gave a soft glow to the wide porch.

Pots of blooming flowers lined the three steps. A swing half-filled with colorful pillows hung at one end of the porch. Two white rocking chairs and more potted plants lined the other side.

The house looked as if it should belong to a family, not a feisty, single professional like Collette. He hesitated before he knocked, listening for voices. The house was silent. He rang the doorbell and waited. No response. Either she wasn't home or didn't want to see him.

Still, he couldn't quite dismiss the figure he'd thought he'd seen running from the house. That left him with an uneasy feeling, and he'd learned it was always best to trust his instincts for danger. One of his commanding officers had claimed that Dylan sniffed out trouble the way a bomb dog trailed the scent of explosives.

His muscles tensed and he hammered his fist against the door. "Collette? Are you in there?"

He called her name again as he turned the knob and the door swung open. He stepped inside. The foyer opened into a dimly lit living room. The illumination came from a lamp and a cluster of candles resting in a copper dish. Magazines were scattered about the sofa, and a glass of wine sat on the coffee table. Nothing was amiss.

"Collette?" he called again. "It's Dylan Ledger. Are you here?"

His call went unanswered.

Lights were on in the back of the house, but all was quiet. He started down the hall. And then he saw the blood. Just a trickle, creeping past an open doorway ahead of him. Curses and panic rattled his skull as he followed the crimson trail into the kitchen.

And to the body lying face down in the middle of the floor.

Chapter Four

The body was not Collette's. Relief merged with dread as Dylan studied the scene.

The victim was fully clothed in jeans and a UT T-shirt. Blood oozed from a cut on the back of the head. A golf-ball-size knot had swelled around it. The blood that spilled across the floor came from a stab wound to the woman's right shoulder, but the bleeding that must have spurted at first had all but stopped.

A bloodied knife lay a few feet from the body. A small skillet stood on its edge against a table leg.

Dylan knelt to check for a pulse. It was rapid, but weak. Her skin lacked the clamminess and paleness that indicated shock, but other than the uneven and shallow rise and fall of her back, she wasn't moving or responding.

Afraid to chance compounding her injuries or starting the bleeding all over again, he left her on her stomach as he took out his phone and called 911. Thankfully, telling the 911 operator to send an ambulance and law enforcement to the old Callister place near the Mustang Run Baptist Church was all the address he needed to give.

"You're okay," Dylan whispered as he covered her with a checkered cloth he'd yanked from the table. "I've called for an ambulance."

She wasn't worried. She was out cold.

Possibilities raced through his mind. Had that been her attacker Dylan had seen running from the scene? Or could the killer still be in the house? He might even be holding Collette hostage.

Dylan struggled to stay calm so that he could weigh the options. He should have paid more attention when Collette had talked of the lowlife who was harassing her. He should have asked questions. Should have…

Hindsight. Always 20/20 and totally worthless.

Muscles tense and hard as stone, he stepped to the counter and took a clean knife from the block.

Leaving the kitchen, he explored the rest of the house, room by room. There were two bedrooms, two baths and a small, uncluttered office. One of the bedrooms had clothes spilling from an open piece of luggage. The other was neat except that the yellow shirt Collette had been wearing today was draped over a wooden rocker.

There was no more blood and no sign of Collette. He went back to the kitchen and checked on the victim. She was still breathing, but still out.

He heard the hum of a motor and the crunch of tires as a vehicle pulled onto the driveway, the same way the attacker must have heard him when he drove up.

Dylan rushed to the front door and spotted Collette exiting her Jeep. Alone and safe. Suddenly his body felt as if he'd been released from a killing chokehold.

He opened the door and waited for her.

"Dylan. I wasn't expecting you."

"I took you up on your invitation to stop by anytime."

"Eleanor must have let you in. I was afraid she'd gone home when she didn't answer the phone. I guess she told you I was working a wedding tonight."

"I haven't talked to Eleanor."

"Then who let you in?"

There was no good way to tell her this. "There's a problem, Collette."

A siren sounded in the distance.

"What kind of problem?"

"An attack."

"On whom?" Her eyes widened. "Where's Eleanor?"

"In the kitchen. She's hurt. I've called an ambulance. They should be—"

Collette bolted toward the kitchen. He followed her, feeling helpless when she went ghostly white and fell to her knees beside her friend.

"Eleanor. Eleanor, say something. Who did this to you? Talk to me. Please talk to me."

"I've called 911." As the wail of the sirens grew louder, Dylan knelt beside her and explained what he knew and how he'd come to find the body.

She shuddered and leaned against him. He put his arm across her shoulders, feeling awkward. He'd never handled emotion well.

She pulled away as the ambulance stopped in front of the house and a rush of footsteps sounded on her front porch. "It was him, Dylan."

"Who?"

Her eyes were moist, but her tone was harsh and accusing. "The man who keeps calling me. He must have come here looking for me, but he found Eleanor instead."

"I wouldn't jump to conclusions." He stood and tugged her to her feet as the room filled with paramedics. By the time they had Eleanor inside the ambulance, more sirens sounded and two squad cars arrived on the scene.

Four armed men in khaki uniforms got out.

Two of the deputies had guns pulled, both aimed at Dylan. For the first time, it hit him that he'd put himself into a very compromising position.

The oldest uniformed man glared at him before stepping between him and Collette. "What happened here?"

"My friend Eleanor was spending the night with me. Someone broke in and attacked her while I was photographing Isabelle Smith's wedding. She was hit at least once on the head and stabbed with one of my kitchen knives. The ambulance just left. They're taking her to the hospital."

"Did she name her attacker?"

"She was unconscious. She'll be afraid when she comes to. I need to go to the hospital so that I can be with her."

"You'll need to answer a few questions first."

Dylan stepped forward. "I'm the one who found the body. I can probably tell you more about the situation than Collette can."

The man turned toward him. "Who the hell are you?"

"Dylan Ledger."

The lawman rested his hand on the butt of his holstered gun. "And I'm Sheriff Glenn McGuire, so you better have a damn good explanation for what you're doing in my daughter's house."

COLLETTE CRINGED at her father's reaction to Dylan. Could he for once just listen to the facts before going off half-cocked?

"Dylan is here because I invited him here."

"I hope you have a hell of a good reason for doing something that stupid."

"Did you ever think that he might have saved Eleanor's life by arriving when he did? He may have saved mine, as well."

"Right now I'm thinking how the Ledgers are back in town one day and we already have a brutal attack. What's Eleanor's last name?"

"Baker. Eleanor Baker. You've met her before, Dad. She visited our house frequently when we were in college."

The sheriff rubbed his chin. "Eleanor? Isn't that the reporter who writes about ghosts?"

"Yes."

"I warned you about hanging out with the likes of her and Melinda Kingston. Kooks attract other kooks. One day you're gonna start listening to me."

Dylan walked over to stand next to Collette and slipped a hand to the small of her back. "You might want to cut Collette some slack, Sheriff. It's rough enough that her friend was attacked."

"I don't need advice from the offspring of a murdering son of a bitch." He turned back to

Collette. "Do you know of anyone who had it in for her?"

Collette took a deep breath. "I don't think she was the intended victim. I think the man was here because of me."

His brows arched. "Why would anyone want to hurt you?"

"I'm not sure that's what he intended, but some man has been calling and harassing me over the past few months. He claims to be in love with me, but I don't even know him."

The sheriff glared at Collette. "You've been stalked by a psycho for months and you never bothered to mention it to me?"

"He never threatened to hurt me."

She couldn't tell if it was anger or frustration that pulled her father's face into deep lines and caused the veins in his face and neck to pop out.

"I should have told you," she said, "but you've told me before that there's not much you can do if there's no threat of violence."

"Did you at least change your phone number when he started calling?"

"I couldn't very well do that. My cell is the only number clients have to reach me. It's on my business cards and my Web site."

"Did he always call you on your cell phone?" the sheriff asked.

"Always."

"Let me see the phone."

"It won't help," Collette said, handing the phone to her father. "The caller ID always said Unavailable or Out of Area."

The sheriff checked out the phone before handing it back to her.

"There are only two vehicles parked outside," the sheriff said.

"Eleanor's car must be in the garage. Mine would be, too, except that I stopped out front when I saw Dylan's truck."

"Check the garage, Brent," he told one of the deputies. "Be nice if the perp stole the victim's car, so we'd have a known vehicle to chase." Sheriff McGuire turned to Dylan. "Where was Eleanor when you arrived?"

"Facedown on the kitchen floor."

The sheriff led the way with the deputies a step behind. Dylan and Collette followed.

"Don't let my father intimidate you," she whispered to him.

"Don't give it a thought. As long as he goes after the lunatic attacker, the rest is insignificant."

She liked Dylan more by the second.

Her father stepped over the stream of blood. "Tell me exactly what you found."

Dylan described the scene as best he could.

The sheriff stooped to get a better look at the

knife and the skillet as he listened. When he'd heard enough, he stood and rocked back on the heels of his boots.

Brent joined them in the kitchen. "There's a blue Ford Mustang in the garage."

"That's Eleanor's," Collette said.

The sheriff nodded. "Brent, wake up the CSI team and tell them I want a full workup on the scene. Chuck, put the state patrol on alert. Tell them we've got a dangerous nut on the loose and may need some help tracking him down. He can't have gotten too far away from this location yet."

"I'm on it," the middle-aged deputy said.

"Good. I'll get with them shortly with whatever pertinent details we can come up with. The rest of you stand guard here and make sure none of the evidence is tampered with until we get prints and any other evidence they can find."

The men jumped to do his bidding.

"We'll talk on the porch," her father said to Collette. "I need more information on your stalker before you leave for the hospital. And, Ledger, don't even think of cutting out before I get through with you."

DYLAN STOOD AT THE EDGE of the porch staring at the scene that had completely changed since he'd arrived at Collette's less than half an hour ago. The quiet had evolved into a chaotic grind of activity, talk and barked orders.

The "ifs" and "buts" of the situation roared though his mind with the same frenetic energy. If he'd left the bar a few minutes earlier, he might have arrived in time to save Eleanor from being attacked. If he'd chased down the figure running from the house, he might have caught the bastard. If Collette had arrived a few minutes earlier, she might have been the one assaulted.

Collette collapsed onto the porch swing and wrapped her arms around her chest although the night was warm. He turned toward her, struck by how incredibly vulnerable she looked.

She hadn't fallen apart even in the first shock of seeing her friend's condition, but she looked as if she was on the verge of it now.

She needed a pair of strong arms wrapped around her, but probably not his. Her father had made it plain that Dylan was the outsider here, persona not grata just by virtue of who he was.

"I should have never let Eleanor spend the night. If she'd driven back to Austin after we left your ranch, she wouldn't have been hurt."

Dylan thought it best not to point out the possible fallacy of that statement. Collette was certain that the man who'd made the disturbing phone calls to her was behind the violence. That wasn't necessarily so. Eleanor might have enemies of her own.

He leaned against the support post near the edge of the steps. "How well did you know Eleanor?"

"We've been best friends since college. The two of us and Melinda Kingston met our first year at UT. We hit it off from the get-go. The three of us shared an off-campus apartment from our sophomore year right through graduation."

"Where does Melinda live now?"

"In Austin, in the same apartment complex as Eleanor. Along with their regular jobs, Melinda and Eleanor are the editors and owners of *Beyond the Grave.* I was helping them out when I met Eleanor at your ranch today."

"Is Eleanor married? Divorced? In a relationship?"

"Not married and no steady relationship. She's a workaholic and a much-sought-after freelance investigative reporter. She'll do whatever it takes to get her story."

And that kind of fervor likely earned her all kinds of enemies, he thought. "Any particular reason why she stayed overnight instead of driving back to Austin?"

"She was interviewing a man just outside Mustang Run early tomorrow morning. She thought it would be easier to just stay here instead of driving back to Austin. She hadn't counted on running into a lunatic."

Not in what seemed to be a quiet, rural Texas town. It had probably seemed even quieter and more peaceful almost eighteen years ago when Dylan's mother had been murdered in similar fashion mere miles away. That time the perpetrator had used a gun.

Damn!

He'd been doing a good job of keeping his own dark memories out of this, but now that he'd acknowledged them, they slunk into his consciousness like a pack of howling coyotes. But this wasn't about the past or him.

"I know you're going to the hospital to see Eleanor, but I don't think you should come back here by yourself after that."

"I live here."

"That doesn't mean you have to spend the night here tonight."

She put her foot flat on the porch to stop the gentle swaying of the swing. "Are you suggesting I stay at your ranch?"

He'd definitely not been suggesting that. "Haunted houses make for a lousy night's sleep," he said, keeping it light.

She shrugged. "I'll be fine, and once my father gets tired of interrogating you, you should go home and get some sleep."

He should. He probably wouldn't. "Your father obviously doesn't approve of our being friends."

"He seldom approves of anything I do. I like it that way."

And yet she still lived on his turf, in the same small town she'd grown up in.

She pulled her cell phone from the pocket of her full skirt. "I should call Melinda. She'll want to know about the assault. And then she can get in touch with Eleanor's mother in Houston."

He nodded and waited.

By the time she broke the connection, he could see new frustrations setting in. "Was there a problem?"

"Melinda was spaced-out on her migraine drugs. She insisted she call Eleanor's mother and she offered to call a cab and go to the hospital, but I told her to stay home. She's a zombie when those headaches set in."

He walked over and dropped to the swing next to Collette. She rested her head on his shoulder and his need to pull her into his arms jumped into overdrive.

This was not the time to have these feelings. And Collette was definitely not the woman to be having them for. It was also not the time to be a jerk, so he slipped a comforting arm around her.

The front door swung open, and the sheriff

stepped onto the porch. He stood like a stone statue, scowling as if he'd caught them in some immoral act. His censure of Dylan couldn't have been clearer.

Screw him, Dylan thought. Yet he stood and moved away from the swing.

The sheriff continued to stare him down. "I have plenty of questions for you, Dylan Ledger, but first I want to hear from my daughter."

The sheriff walked to the edge of the porch and spit a wad of tobacco into the dirt before turning to Collette. "What do you know about this stalker and why haven't you come to me about this before now?"

Chapter Five

Her reasoning seemed futile now. Could it be that she'd let Eleanor face this because of her own stubborn resentment toward her father?

Collette took a deep breath and tried to put her guilt aside for now. She needed her full powers of concentration to recall every detail she'd gleaned from the madman's phone calls. That was the least she could do for Eleanor.

She clasped her hands in her lap. "I didn't come to you because the man's calls were never threatening. At first I thought they were a joke."

"A joke? Someone was stalking you and you took it for a joke?"

"At first," she admitted. "He'd say how beautiful I was and that he couldn't get me out of his mind. I figured one of my friends had put him up to it."

"What else did he say?"

"I can't remember word for word. The first few times, it was as if he was flirting. He'd say how much he looked forward to meeting me. When I asked why he didn't tell me who he was, he'd say he was waiting for the right time."

"I take it that progressed."

"Yes. A few weeks ago, he started freaking me out. He'd describe how I looked in a specific dress or outfit, talk about how I'd worn my hair, comment on the errands I'd run that day. He seemed to know everything about me, what I did, where I went. That made me increasingly nervous."

"But he never asked you to meet him?"

"Not once, though he kept saying we'd meet soon and that I'd like him."

"What about his voice? Did it remind you of anyone you know?"

"No, that was the creepiest part of the calls. His voice sounded strained, croaky, as if he had a perpetual case of laryngitis. I'd recognize that voice anywhere. That's why I'm almost sure I've never met him."

"When did this start?"

"A few months back."

"Be more specific."

"Sometime around mid-March, I think. I was working late in my studio." She'd taken it so lightly that first time, but it made her skin crawl now to think that even that night he might have been snooping around, watching her every move.

"Damn it, Colley. What were you thinking? You should have called me immediately."

Colley. He'd reverted to his childhood name for her. She'd hated it, thought it made her sound like a dog. Eventually, he'd dropped it, but tonight it felt right.

He started to pace. "Think, Colley. Had you met someone new who'd come on to you, maybe while photographing a wedding or a party of some kind?"

"No."

"Are you sure?"

"How can I be sure? People talk to me all the time. I don't think about the possibility that they could be stalkers."

"Don't get riled with me. I'm just asking."

"I know. I'm sorry. This is just so hard when I don't even know how badly Eleanor is injured."

But her father's questions kept coming, on and on until her head felt as if someone were pushing needles into her brain.

When she could take no more, she buried her face in her hands and tried to regroup. She knew her father needed something specific to go on, but there was no consistent pattern to the stalker's calls. All she knew of the man was his voice and the way it had started to creep inside her stomach and turn it into knots whenever he'd call.

Drowning in guilt wouldn't help. She gripped

the chains that held the swing and raised her head, finally looking at her father. "I realize now that I should have reported the phone calls, but I've heard you say yourself that there's little law enforcement can do when an unidentified stalker fails to make physical threats."

"I'm your father, Collette. I would have found a way to track down the son of a bitch."

"Then do it now," she said, her nerves stretched to the breaking point.

"Your daughter's had a rough night," Dylan said, interrupting the conversation for the first time since her father had started grilling her. "Maybe you should give the questions a rest for now."

"When I want your advice, I'll ask for it, Ledger."

His continuous brusque treatment of Dylan was uncalled for, and it grated on Collette's already raw nerves. "Dylan's right, Dad. I'll keep trying to think of anything I can to help, but we're wasting time here and Eleanor might need me."

Her dad nodded and spit again, wiping his mouth on his sleeve before walking over to the swing where she was sitting. "Okay, but I don't feel good about you being alone while the lunatic who attacked Eleanor is still on the loose."

"I won't be alone. I'm going straight to the hospital."

"Get your things and Brent can drive you there. When you're finished, he can take you to Bill and Alma's to spend the rest of the night."

Always with the orders. But this time she would do as he said—or almost as he said. "I'll take my own car. I don't like being stuck anywhere without it."

"Dumb move with a lunatic on the loose who has made it his business to follow you around. But if you insist on having your car, Brent can drive you to the hospital and I'll have one of the other deputies drive your car to Bill's."

"Okay." Too bad Dylan hadn't invited her to his place for the night. Her father would have thrown a fit, but it would have been a lot easier than going over all of this again with her brother and his wife.

And she really hated the thought of bringing Georgia into this. Not that they could keep it from her. Nothing stayed secret in Mustang Run.

When she stood to go inside, her father put a hand on her shoulder. The touch was discomfiting for her and no doubt for him, as well. She'd accepted long ago that he was guarded with his emotions. Instead he gave orders and criticized.

And drove away the best things in his life.

"We'll get the son of a bitch, Colley." He patted

her on the shoulder and then stepped back. "You get your things together. I'll go tell Brent the plan."

When he walked away, Dylan took his place at her side and took her hands in his. "None of this is your fault, Collette. Don't let anyone make you think that it is."

There was no awkwardness in Dylan's touch. He was practically a stranger, yet it was easier to turn to him for comfort than to her own father.

"Thanks," she murmured. "For everything."

"Glad I could help."

"Keep that thought while my father is trying to break you the way he would a wild steed. That's what you get for coming to the aid of the sheriff's daughter."

"I'm not worried about him, but I can see why he's suspicious about my showing up here tonight. Just for the record, why did you tell me to stop by anytime?"

She had no answer that made sense even to her. "I guess I just wanted to see you again." She pushed through the door, then stopped and turned back to face Dylan. "Why did you come?"

"Two beers. Dread of going back to the ranch." He leaned against the door frame. "And I wanted to see you again."

She could really grow to like this man.

DYLAN WOKE and opened his eyes at the smell of brewing coffee drifting from the kitchen. The predawn darkness outside his window told him daybreak was at least a half hour away. He couldn't have slept more than a few hours.

Punching his pillow, he rolled to his stomach. A pain attacked just below the small of his back. The mattress on his boyhood bed was likely the culprit, either that or the strain of the previous evening.

He'd assumed it would be the memories of his past that messed up his mind when he returned to Mustang Run. Now there were new dilemmas to consume his thoughts and rob him of sleep.

The only good news was that Collette had called him from the hospital last night to let him know that her friend Eleanor had regained consciousness and was in stable condition, though too groggy from pain medication to answer questions.

She'd suffered a concussion and needed to undergo surgery today to repair damage to her shoulder. But luckily the injuries were not life-threatening.

Nonetheless, Collette sounded panicky about her friend's condition.

The floorboards squeaked when he threw his legs over the side of the bed and planted his size-ten feet. Fatigue still clung to him like soap scum to a shower door, but he might as well face the day ahead and his dad.

Dylan grabbed the jeans he'd worn yesterday from the chair where he'd tossed them last night. He'd shower and change after coffee. He didn't bother with shoes or a shirt. He did stop at the bathroom, take care of business, wash his hands and rake his damp fingers through his hair.

When he stepped into the kitchen, his dad was standing at the back door looking out and seemingly studying the skulking shadows made by branches swaying in the slight breeze.

"You're up early," Troy said, not bothering to turn around.

"I smelled coffee."

"Yeah. I started a pot once I figured out how. Even appliances have changed a lot in seventeen years."

Dylan hadn't considered that there would be so many common everyday things his father hadn't done while he was in prison. Even moving around his own kitchen must seem strange.

That was another reason Dylan probably should have given him some time to adjust on his own before barging in as a welcoming party of one. But the attorney had felt it important that at least one of Troy's sons be there for his homecoming.

"You were out late last night," Troy said.

Dylan nodded. When the coffee indicator flashed green, he took two mugs from the cabinet and filled both of them, handing one to his father.

"No place better to party than Texas," Troy said.

"Actually I was late because I ran into a problem."

The tension factor in the room increased. "What kind of problem?"

"A young woman was viciously attacked. I was the first one on the scene."

Troy winced as if the words had been blows. His free hand clenched and unclenched a couple of times before he pulled a chair from the kitchen table and sat down.

"It won't involve you," Dylan said. "I can handle this on my own. I've already explained all I know to the sheriff. I just wanted you to know what's going on."

"Sheriff Glenn McGuire?"

"Afraid so. I think he's a fixture in Mustang Run."

"One that should have been replaced and junked years ago. How about starting at the beginning and telling me how and where you stumbled upon this crime?"

Dylan joined him at the table, though he'd have preferred to stand and occasionally pace. He'd been diagnosed with ADHD a few years after his mother had died. He'd supposedly outgrown the problem, but sitting still when his mind was going a mile a minute remained a challenge for him.

Dylan went over the details, leaving nothing out. By the time he'd finished, the situation seemed far more confusing than it had last night.

Troy worried a small glass saltshaker that had been left on the table from the night before. "If the stalker knew as much about Collette as his calls indicated, then he surely wouldn't have mistaken Eleanor Baker for her."

"That's just one of the factors that don't make sense."

"What are the others?"

"Motivation for breaking and entering and assaulting the friend of someone you claim is your soul mate."

"I'm sure Glenn McGuire is way ahead of you on that."

No doubt. Dylan sipped the hot brew while he tried to refit the puzzle in his mind. "It's possible the perpetrator wasn't Collette's stalker," he said, thinking out loud. "The man might have been after Eleanor."

Troy leaned forward and propped his elbows on the table. "Or it could have been just a random attack of violence. But you said Eleanor had re-gained consciousness. She may be able to clear this up."

"Hopefully soon, but last I heard she was too woozy from pain meds and too weak to question. What worries me most is if the man who's been making the harassing phone calls to Collette is responsible for the attack, he is one sick bastard."

"Or just a normal man who snapped," Troy said. "It happens."

The same way people said it had happened with Troy when he'd killed Dylan's mother. "I don't agree that normal people just snap into violence," Dylan said, needing to get that much off his chest. "Losing control is just another form of cop-out. But if Collette's stalker is guilty of the attack, then Collette is in real danger."

"Her father's the sheriff. I'm sure he realizes that and has the resources to keep her safe until the nutcase is apprehended."

Meaning Collette wasn't Dylan's responsibility. He got that. It didn't do much for relieving the anxiety that was eating away at him now.

"I'll get some more coffee," Dylan said, need-ing a break. He took their mugs to the counter and refilled both of them.

Troy hunched over his cup. "Tell me exactly what the sheriff said when he questioned you alone, Dylan. Word for word or as close as you can remember it."

"There's not that much to tell. Most of the questions were redundant and a waste of time."

"He was hoping you'd mutter something he could use against you."

"I'm not a suspect, Dad. He might wish I was, but he's got nothing on me."

"Don't underestimate Glenn McGuire. Did he question you about your reasons for being at Collette's?"

"Yeah, and he clearly didn't like that his daughter was mixed up with a Ledger."

"Did he ask about your personal life?"

"For an hour, but other than a couple of speeding tickets, I'm clean as a whistle. Besides, if there's any doubt about me in the sheriff's mind, Eleanor will clear that up as soon as she can talk."

Any question of his guilt was a nonissue in Dylan's mind, but Troy was growing increasingly agitated. The muscles in his bare arms bunched as if he were about to slug someone.

"Get a lawyer, Dylan. Today. Before the sheriff comes calling with more questions."

"There's no call for me to get lawyered up. I didn't do anything wrong."

"Guilt or innocence doesn't matter to McGuire. He makes his own rules. The evidence is what he says it is. Take my word for it. You need an attorney."

His father's reaction was too intense for this to just be about last night. It had to track back to Troy's experiences. Was he convinced that the sheriff had built a murder case against him when no evidence existed?

If so, his anger and frustration were justified.

"You need an experienced attorney who's on top of his game," Troy said. "I'll ask Able Drake. He'll know who's who in the legal world."

"I appreciate the offer, but I can't afford that kind of counsel. And I don't need it. If anything, I'm the hero here. I may have frightened off the attacker before he finished the job of killing Eleanor and then waited around for Collette."

He could tell by the look on his father's face that he wasn't convinced by Dylan's logic.

Troy pushed back from the table. "At least give it some thought. Now, how about some bacon and eggs?"

"That, I could use."

His father broke some eggs into a bowl while Dylan peeled the bacon from the package and fit it into the frying pan. He surveyed the refrigerator and found butter and blackberry preserves.

Whoever Able Drake was, he'd done a good job of getting the cupboard stocked and the house ready. If it turned out Dylan needed an attorney, he'd keep Able in mind. But he didn't expect to need one.

"Did the sheriff give you any warnings, like not to leave the state or the county until he gave you clearance?" Troy asked, obviously not quite ready to drop the subject.

"Only one, and it was more an order than a warning."

"What was that?"

"Stay away from his daughter."

COLLETTE'S BROTHER grabbed a hot biscuit from the pan his wife had just taken from the oven, juggling it until it was cool enough to handle. He took the seat that was catty-corner from Collette at the table. "Did you eat, Sis?"

"No. My stomach would rebel."

"You look worn. You should go back to bed and catch a few more z's."

"I couldn't sleep."

"Exhaustion won't help anyone."

"You couldn't have gotten much sleep yourself. You were still up when I arrived during the wee hours of the morning."

"I'd been asleep. Dad talked to Brent when you two left the hospital. He called here and wanted me to make sure you got here safely and didn't leave again."

"Good old Dad."

"He doesn't want you seeing Dylan Ledger again. I agree. Stay away from him."

Alma joined them in the kitchen, still in her robe but with her bobbed brown hair combed and her make-up on. "Bill, do you have lunch money for Georgia? The smallest bill I have is a twenty."

"I gave her enough for the week on Monday."

"She had to pay for some supplies she needed for art class."

"Lunch money is for lunch."

"And while you're at it, I need money for Sukey."

"The cleaning woman's fees are supposed to come out of your household budget."

Alma went to the pitcher of fresh-squeezed orange juice and poured herself a glass, ignoring his complaints. Bill pulled out his wallet and divvied up the money, ones for Georgia, twenties for Alma to pay Sukey. He was dressed impeccably, blue-striped suit and silk tie in a muted pattern, standard attire for the insurance company he owned and managed in Mustang Run.

"Thanks for letting me barge in on you in the middle of the night," Collette said.

"Glad to have you," Alma said. "The extra bedroom is yours for as long as you want it."

"I appreciate that." Actually she'd already stayed as long as she wanted. It wasn't that she had issues with her brother. It was more that they weren't from the same planet. He was all about rules and routine and handing out advice. Not as adamant as their father was, but enough so that Collette with her free-spirited approach to life was never totally in her comfort zone at his house.

She liked Alma, but there was a disconnect factor there, as well. On the other hand, Collette absolutely adored her niece. Georgia was not only intelligent and outgoing, she was energetic and upbeat.

"I'm playing tennis at the country club this morning," Alma said. "Why don't you join us, Collette? The exercise and fresh air will do you good. I mean, if there's nothing you can do for your friend who was attacked."

"I need to clean my kitchen."

Alma made a face. "You don't want to clean up blood. If I ask, I'm sure Sukey can fit you in this week. I have a key to your house that I can let her use. That way you can put last night's incident behind you."

Last night's "incident," as if Eleanor's near-fatal assault was a spilled drink or a bit of vomit that had soaked into the carpet.

Georgia picked that minute to walk into the kitchen, her school backpack slung over one shoulder. She tossed it onto an empty chair.

"Good. You're awake, Aunt Collette." She gave Collette a quick hug. "Dad told me about what happened when he got me up for school. You must be bummed to the max."

"To the max," Collette agreed.

"I'm really sorry. Was the woman who was attacked the woman you were going to meet when I saw you after school yesterday?"

"She was."

"Dad said Grandpa will get the man who attacked her."

Collette wondered what else her brother had told Georgia about the attack. He hadn't wanted to tell her anything, but Collette had persuaded him that it was better coming from one of them than from the kids at school. News of violence traveled fast in a tight-knit community like Mustang Run.

"It's okay if you can't take me shopping this week," Georgia said, "but I hope you can make the party on Saturday."

"I wouldn't miss it."

"Are you afraid that man might break into your house again? Is that why you're staying with us?"

Bill brushed a crumb from the front of his shirt. "Stop bugging your aunt, Georgia. Grab you lunch money and your book bag and I'll give you a lift to school."

Georgia gave Collette another quick hug and her mother a peck on the cheek before following Bill to the car.

"She's a good kid," Collette said.

"But impressionable," Alma added. "The less she hears about the brutality the better. I know she'll question you, but—"

"I never planned to go into the gritty details with her," Collette interrupted, irritated that Alma might think she would. "I'm going to get dressed and then I'll get out of your hair."

Her cell phone rang as she started back to the guest room. Melinda's name came up on the caller ID. Collette ducked into the room and closed the door before taking the call.

"I'm glad you called," Collette said. "Have you heard from Eleanor this morning?"

"I just got off the phone with Mrs. Baker. She said they'll be taking Eleanor into surgery any minute. I offered to come up and sit with Mrs. Baker, but she said it wasn't necessary."

"Is Eleanor talking?"

"Very little. Her mother says she's still confused about what happened to her. The doctor thinks it's likely due to the pain medication."

"I'm sure my father is driving them crazy wanting to question her about the attack."

"Your father is the real reason I called. Can you give him a message for me? He gave me his cell-phone number, but I can't remember what I did with it."

"Sure. What's the message?"

"I located the two articles he asked about."

"What articles?"

"Ones that Eleanor wrote about the Ledger murder and trial. I can fax them to him if he'll give me a fax number."

Collette sank to the bed. "My father called you this morning to ask about those?"

"Yes, but I don't mind. I told him that I want to help find the man who tried to kill Eleanor in any way I can."

Collette's stomach churned. How dare he do this? "The Ledgers have nothing to do with last night's attack on Eleanor."

"I hope you're right, but with Dylan's being there and Troy Ledger just getting out of prison, I can see why Sheriff McGuire wants to check this out."

So could Collette, and a surge of anger whipped though her like a riled rattlesnake.

"I'll give Dad the message, Melinda."

When they broke the connection, Collette yanked a pair of jeans and a teal-blue pullover sweater from the duffle she'd thrown together last night. She dressed quickly, gave her disheveled mass of hair a couple of careless brushes and tinged her lips with gloss.

"Where are you going in such a rush?" Alma asked when Collette passed her in the hallway.

"To pay a visit to Dylan Ledger. Be sure and tell my father that if he calls."

Chapter Six

It was just after eight in the morning when Dylan stepped out the back door. The sky was cloudless, and already the sun was warm on his back. He walked toward the old storage building just behind the garage.

Mockingbirds were having a lively banter in the branches of the mulberry tree just past the back steps. A spattering of weedy yellow wildflowers he couldn't name dotted the pasture that stretched into the distance.

It was a typical, serene pastoral scene, but the thoughts playing havoc with Dylan's mind were anything but tranquil. Collette McGuire was at the center of his mental chaos. He wasn't sure if her stalker had anything to do with the attack, but he couldn't shake the feeling that she was in danger.

The good sheriff didn't want Dylan anywhere near his daughter. Not that Dylan would lose sleep over what Glenn McGuire wanted. He would stay away from Collette, but only because she didn't need him. The sheriff was a hotheaded, arrogant blowhard, but he was in the perfect position to protect Collette.

Dylan would only bring complications and excess baggage to the table. The murderer's kid all over again. Obviously, some things never changed.

Standing around stressing over a situation he could do nothing about wasn't helping, either, he told himself. He might as well take a drive around the ranch and see what kind of work his father was looking at if he actually planned to get the spread up and running again.

Not that his father had asked for or given any indication that he wanted Dylan's input. He'd left while Dylan was in the shower with not so much as a scribbled note as to where he was going or when he'd be back.

Before Dylan reached his truck, he heard the rumble of a vehicle bumping its way along the rutted ranch road. He recognized Collette's Jeep the second it came into sight. A surge of unwelcome anticipation pulsated along his nerve endings.

By the time she'd come to a complete stop, he was opening her door for her. She jumped out, eyes blazing as if she were showing up for a gunfight.

It worried him how much he wanted to pull her into his arms. Instead he closed the door after her. "More trouble?" he asked.

"For you."

He tensed a little. "Care to explain?"

"My father's out to get you."

So her concern was for him. He relaxed a little, even liking the fact that she'd gotten this fired up on his account.

"Is he bringing his rope over to hang me?"

"More likely his gun to shoot you in the back, and this isn't funny, Dylan."

He found it amazing that she could be that angry and look that good. "I'm not amused. I'm just thankful you weren't upset about something more serious."

"You don't think involving you in a felony is serious enough?"

"The sheriff is just blowing off steam because he doesn't like the fact that you invited a Ledger to your house. As soon as Eleanor talks, he'll have to eat crow."

"You do not know my father. He called my friend Melinda this morning wanting her to look up some articles that Eleanor had written about your mother's murder."

At least he wasn't going around town leading the chorus of "murderer's kid." "If I went around attacking every journalist who'd ever written about our family, I'd be busy from morning until night."

"That's not the point."

"So, what is the point? That your father doesn't like me? Big deal. That he thinks all Ledgers should be hung on general principle? He's probably not the only one of that opinion."

"But he's not just someone with an opinion. He's the sheriff and he has no conscience when it comes to destroying people."

"Is this still about me? Because it sounds a lot like personal father bashing."

"I'm trying to warn you about him."

"I'm not afraid of your father, Collette."

"You should be."

He stepped to his truck and opened the passenger-side door for her. "Get in."

"Why? Where are we going?"

"For a ride around the ranch and a chance for you to cool down so that we can talk about this rationally." He stepped back. "Unless you agree with your father and you're afraid to go off with me."

"If I were afraid of you, Dylan Ledger, I wouldn't be standing here right now." She climbed into the truck to prove her point. "But I do need to call and cancel my appointments for the day." She pulled a day planner out of her handbag and started making calls.

She might not be afraid of him, but he was afraid of her. Afraid of falling for a woman in a town that had spit him out years ago and showed no signs of wanting him back. He didn't mind playing bad boy, but he wasn't going to spend a lifetime sticking out his face just to get his teeth kicked in.

He climbed behind the wheel. She leaned forward and her gorgeous red hair tumbled in front of her, falling over her spectacular breasts. She threw back her head and shoved a tangle of curls behind her ears. Her green eyes sparkled like fiery emeralds when she looked up to find him staring at her.

"Are we going to sit here all day, or are you going to drive?"

Man, did he hate gorgeous, feisty redheads with svelte bodies and killer smiles. If he told himself that enough, he might even start to believe it sometime.

About the time he believed that Texas was going to secede from the Union and bulls were really sweet-natured creatures who'd just gotten a bum rap.

COLLETTE BUCKLED HER seat belt as Dylan shifted into Drive and gunned the accelerator. Fifty yards past the house, the ranch road became little more than tire grooves cut into the hard, dry earth. Overgrown pastures and broken fences stretched endlessly in front of them. They were totally alone.

If she had any fear of Dylan, it would surely surface now. But there was none. She knew next to nothing about him yet she'd felt a connection with him almost from the moment he'd arrived at the ranch. She'd hoped he'd call, had been excited when she'd seen his truck parked in front of her house last night.

Admittedly, he was cocky and a bit arrogant and even had a cowboy swagger about him, though his hands were too smooth to belong to a rancher. Yet he'd been protective and sensitive last night, supportive, but not overwhelming.

Dylan lowered the driver's window and propped his arm on the door. "It's been five years since anyone's run cattle out here and it shows."

"I didn't realize anyone had been here since your father…"

"Since he went to prison? You can say it, Collette. I won't be offended by the truth."

"Sorry. It just seemed callous to put it so bluntly."

"No one's lived in the house," he explained, "but a man named Tom Hartwell rented the land. I'm assuming he used it for cattle. I don't see any signs it's been used for anything else."

"I know the Hartwells. His wife cuts hair at a

salon on Main Street. Tom lost his arm in a hay-baling accident about five years ago. I heard he cut way back on his herd after that."

"I never heard that, but guess it explains why he quit renting the pastures of Willow Creek Ranch."

"Some people around here expected one of the Ledger sons to come back to run the ranch once you were grown."

"We talked about it," Dylan admitted, "but neither my brothers nor I were excited about the prospect of living in Mustang Run."

"Does that mean you're not staying?"

"Don't plan to, nor have I been invited. Now that my father's out of prison, the ranch is his to run as he sees fit."

"Do you have a position to go back to?"

"No. I joined the army right after I graduated from the university. When I was discharged six months ago, I gave working for my uncle's advertising agency a shot. The job and I were not a fit. It required far too many hours shut up in an office."

Dylan turned to face her. She met his gaze and felt his penetrating stare vibrate though her. Even with all that had happened over the past few hours, she couldn't escape the fact that he stirred something a bit primeval and feral in her.

Dylan took a left that put them on a dirt road

leading over a crest and then started downhill. "You seem calmer," he said. "Now do you want to talk about what happened last night?"

"I came here to let you know what my father is up to, not to rehash the attack."

"Your father is a smart man, Collette. He may not trust me, but he can't manufacture a case against me. If he's arrogant enough to try, Eleanor Baker will nullify the strategy as soon as she's able to describe her real attacker."

"Assuming she got a good look at the man before he hit her over the head with the skillet."

"I say we go on that assumption until we find out differently. Better yet, let's operate on the assumption that your father has a lead on your stalker by now. I'm sure he's checking your phone records. It's amazing how close they can pinpoint the origin of calls these days."

"If he has valid information, he hasn't given me any of it."

"Have you had any more calls from the stalker?"

"No."

"And there's a good chance you won't. He's likely afraid to call now, for fear the sheriff already has a lead on identifying him."

Dylan stopped beneath an oak tree sporting its new cover of green leaves. A creek that was practically overflowing from the spring rains rushed past them.

"Is this the ranch's namesake?" Collette asked.

"This is it. Willow Creek."

"I don't see any willows."

"There are black willow trees along the northern edge of the creek. My brother Sean and I used to sit beneath them and fish for bream." Dylan opened his door and climbed out of the truck. The scene in front of her was too tempting not to join him.

She walked to the edge of the creek. "Did you ever swim in the creek?"

"We had a better spot for swimming, though I'm not sure I can find it anymore, at least not by truck. None of us boys were driving then, so we went by horseback."

"Is it part of the creek?"

"Better. It's a spring-fed pool, cold year round, but the water felt great in July and August. I got in trouble more than once for sneaking off to swim before I'd finished my chores."

"And I'll bet your brothers were right behind you."

"Wyatt was usually leading the way."

Dylan had known the life every Texas boy dreamed of and then he'd lost that and both parents. One to death. One to prison. It was difficult to believe that after all that, he'd become the confident, easygoing man he seemed today.

"You must have missed life on the ranch terribly when you had to move away."

He shrugged. "For a while. I hated city life. Uncle Phil said I was a cowboy who fell out of the saddle and then lost the horse. At first it made me mad when he said that, but then I figured it was pretty much how things were."

"Who is Uncle Phil?"

"My mom's oldest brother, the one who owns the advertising agency. He and Aunt Sylvie were elected to take me in when my grandparents divvied us up."

That surprised her. "I just assumed you and your brothers went to live with your grandparents."

"Nope. They said five was too many for them to handle, so they shared the wealth. And don't give me that look, Collette. I hate that look."

"What look?"

"That oh-you-poor-dear look. So my life wasn't ideal. Whose is? And that was all years ago."

"Point made." She slipped out of her sandals and rolled up the legs of her jeans. Stepping cautiously to avoid sinking in a muddy spot, she made her way to the edge of the creek.

Slowly she dipped a toe into the water. The cold slapped against her. She stumbled backward.

Dylan's arms wrapped around her and held her

steady. Her breath held at the gentle pressure of his fingers on her stomach and the strong cushion of his chest at her back. She inhaled the musky, woodsy scent of him and something stirred deep inside her, an ache that was both sweet and painful at the same time.

His arms tightened around her, and his lips touched the back of her neck. A tingle danced through her, leaving her weak.

He exhaled slowly and released her. "Gotta watch those slippery slopes."

Too late. She was falling. And it had nothing to do with the water or the mud. She'd just have to make sure she didn't fall so hard she couldn't move on when Dylan left Mustang Run.

Once out of the water, she wiped her damp feet on the thick carpet of grass and then slipped back into her sandals. Dylan waited and walked at her side as they started back to the truck. If the moment of closeness had gotten to him the way it had her, he showed no signs.

Her cell phone rang. Part of her hoped the caller would be her stalker. She'd like to tell him that she knew he'd attacked Eleanor and that he would pay for it. Still, the dread stabbed at her composure as she took the phone from the leather holster attached to her low-riding jeans.

The ID read Dad. The dread turned to fury. She didn't bother with a hello. "Why did you call Melinda this morning and ask her to look up Eleanor's articles on Troy Ledger?"

"I'm working an investigation, Collette. The woman who was attacked is a reporter. I can't rule out the fact that she pissed off somebody and they came after her."

"Not somebody, Dad. You asked about Dylan in particular. I told you this isn't about Eleanor, and it's definitely not about Dylan Ledger. Leave him out of this."

"Don't start telling me how to do my job, Collette. What kind of crazy stunt do you think you're pulling by going to the Ledger ranch?"

"I figured someone should warn Dylan what you were up to."

"You did, did you?" Anger chipped at his words so that each syllable was sharp and spiked.

"Yes. I'm with Dylan now, as a matter of fact."

"I'm not ruling out anyone and you can stop acting like Dylan's attorney. You don't even know the man you're defending and cavorting with. I'm sending Brent to pick you up and drive you back to Bill's."

"I'm not cavorting. And don't bother sending Brent. I'm capable of taking care of myself."

"You're as pigheaded as—"

"You, Dad." She broke the connection before he could say more. Her heart was pounding, but she knew what she had to do. Not for her but for Dylan. He'd been through enough in this town without her father shoveling more crap on top of him.

Dylan opened the truck door for her. "I take it that was the sheriff."

"Yes, and as genial as he always is if someone dares to cross him."

"You don't have to defend me to him, Collette. I fight my own battles, and I don't want to come between you and your father."

"You're way too late in the scheme of things to do that."

She considered her options on the drive back to the Ledger house. Staying with Bill and Alma wasn't the answer. It would only disrupt their lives and Georgia's.

Staying alone in her house and thinking about Eleanor lying facedown in her blood every time she walked into the kitchen didn't sound like a good idea, either.

There was another choice. It would piss off her father, but he'd surely get the message that he couldn't tell her whom she could befriend and whom she should reject.

She shifted so she could face Dylan. "How do you think your father would feel about a house-guest his first week back in Mustang Run?"

"So far, he's not overly excited."

"You're not a guest. You're family."

He shot her a dubious look. "Am I missing something here?"

"My father thinks I need a protector. I'm thinking you'd fit that bill to perfection. You have a big house. I'd stay out of the way. You'd hardly know I was there."

"Your father would go ballistic."

"That's what makes this a win-win."

She'd just have to be careful on those sensual slippery slopes of attraction. Surely she could handle that.

TROY HAD SPENT most of the morning driving aimlessly, down one blacktop road after the other, trying to come to grips with what it meant to be back in Mustang Run. He'd thought he could handle it, but eighteen years had done nothing to erase the pain of losing Helene.

Every detail was still burned into his mind. The choking humidity that had slowed down his progress at setting a new row of fence posts and made him late getting home for lunch. The smell of burned peas. The voice of Mariah Carey singing about love on their old stereo system. Helene had loved Mariah Carey.

He closed his eyes tight as the pictures slipped from their hiding places in his mind and returned to torture him. Helene's beautiful body bloodied and nearly naked stretched out on the living-room floor. Her head was lying on the cold, hard stones of the hearth. Her long, dark hair was matted with her blood.

Life had ended for him that day. He'd kept breathing and walking, going through the motions. But he'd stopped living. His attorney had accused him of not fighting hard enough to prove his innocence during the yearlong ordeal of questioning and trial. The truth was he hadn't fought at all. Dead men had no fight left in them.

He'd let down his sons. Helene would never forgive him that.

He left the old farm-to-market road and turned into a section of town that had been ranch land the last time he'd seen it. Big houses of brick or stucco with two- and sometimes three-car garages filled every lot. Mostly commuters or retirees, he imagined. Mustang Run did not have the jobs to support that style of living.

Leaving the suburbs behind him, he made his way to the old part of town. Main Street had become a strand of antiques shops and coffeehouses. The only establishment that bore any resemblance to a place he remembered was Abby's Diner.

Abby had been working at her father's dry cleaners when Troy moved to Mustang Run to work as a wrangler for the Black Spur Ranch.

He'd dated her a couple of times. They'd never clicked as a couple, but later, after Abby had opened the diner, she and Helene had become good friends.

Troy had mostly roamed the rodeo circuit before settling in Mustang Run, working just enough to earn entrance fees. He'd found the wrangling job through a newspaper ad, and the New York owner of the Black Spur had hired him via a phone call. The guy had taken more interest in using the ranch for a tax write-off than making money.

Troy made him money anyway and that's when ranching had gotten into his blood.

Impulsively, Troy pulled into a parking spot a few stores down and walked to the diner. The smell of coffee, cinnamon and spices greeted him when he stepped though the door.

The chairs at the bar were mostly occupied by older guys, none of whom he recognized. Several looked up, though only one made eye contact. Troy nodded as the chatter in the small diner diminished into an uncomfortable hush.

He made his way to a booth, slid in, removed his Western hat and set it on the seat beside him. The hat felt strange on his head, the same way his new boots and jeans felt, as if he were a pretender who should still be in a prison jumpsuit.

A pretty, slim waitress with a nice smile and

the whitest teeth Troy had ever seen stopped at his elbow. Her badge said her name was Jenny.

"Just coffee?" Jenny asked, when he gave his order. "Abby makes the best biscuits and gravy in town."

So Abby was still around. At least something in this town had stayed the same, other than the arrogant sheriff. "I've already had breakfast," he said. Even then his appetite had been dulled by the new developments with Dylan.

He didn't see the son he remembered when he looked at Dylan. The son he remembered was a scrawny kid who loved to watch cartoons on TV and hated homework. Dylan was a man now—with his mother's eyes.

That got to Troy, made him realize that his sons were all he had left of her. And they were strangers. None of the others had even bothered to contact him since he'd been released from prison. He understood why, but it didn't make it any easier.

"I wondered how long it would take you to face your adoring public."

Troy looked up as Abby wiped her hands on her white apron, slid into the booth across from him and pushed a mug of steaming coffee his way. Evidently, Jenny had reported they had an infamous celebrity in the house.

The years hadn't been nearly as hard on Abby

as they'd been on him. If anything, she looked better than she had before. She'd picked up some weight. Her bones no longer poked at her skin.

"My admirers don't seem all that excited to see me," he said.

"Because they bought into the prosecutor's lies. Your refusal to cooperate with your attorney didn't leave them a lot of choice."

"Let's not go back there."

"Whatever you say." She reached over and straightened the envelopes of sweetener. "I heard Dylan came back to town to help you get settled in."

"Word gets around."

"You don't need Facebook or Twitter to keep up with the gossip in Mustang Run."

"Good. I don't even have a computer as yet."

"I'm glad Dylan came, Troy. The boys need to get to know you. They're older now. They can make up their own minds about you and not have everything filtered through Helene's family."

"I'm not expecting miracles."

"Maybe you should. You're out of prison. That's a miracle in itself."

"You could call it that." And he wouldn't waste the opportunity that provided him. He had a score to settle. He'd never rest easy until he did.

Abby spread her hands palms down on the table. "Sheriff McGuire was in the other day."

"The man probably knows a good cup of coffee when he tastes it."

"You were the topic of his conversation. He's not going to make your return easy on you."

"I wasn't expecting him to throw a party."

"I'm serious, Troy. He said he planned to watch you like a hawk. Cross any line and he'll come down on you like misery on Job."

"I'll keep that in mind."

"Make sure you do."

The bell over the door rang and a middle-aged woman with frizzy brown hair and a rail-thin body stepped into the diner. A tall guy, muscled, with thinning hair and a tattoo on his left bicep, followed her in.

The woman stared openly at Troy before sliding into a booth.

Abby gave her a friendly wave and then leaned across the table. "Do you know who that is?" she asked, keeping her voice low.

"Can't say that I do."

"Edna Granger. You have to remember her. Five or six years younger than us. Wore her sweaters super tight. All the guys had the hots for her."

"I'm guessing I didn't."

"I forgot. Once you met Helene, you didn't know any other woman existed."

"Who's the guy?" Troy asked, making conversation and pretending he cared.

"I have no idea. I've never seen him before, but I can't believe he's a love interest. I've seen corpses that had more life in them than Edna."

"She looks like she's had a tough life," Troy agreed.

"You better believe it. Her husband got gunned down in Brownsville in some kind of drug turf war a couple of years ago. That's when she moved back here. Her addict daughter was shot last fall while she was high on crack cocaine. Losing her only child destroyed what was left of poor Edna."

"Does this story have a point?"

"Edna's lost her daughter and that turned her into a bitter woman. But living with nothing but anger and regret won't bring her daughter back."

He was beginning to see where this was going. He took a long sip of his coffee and waited for it.

"Helene wouldn't want you to give up, Troy. She'd want you to be a father to her sons even if they are grown. She'd want you to keep living and ranching."

"And eating pie?"

"Yes. And eating pie. Just don't dry up like Edna."

He had no intention of drying up, not until the dirty bastard who'd taken Helene's life paid with his own. "Don't worry about me, Abby. I've got things under control."

"If you ever need a friend, my number's in the book."

"I'll keep that in mind."

"I won't be holding my breath. Now I've got to get back to the kitchen before the crusts on my cherry pies turn from gold to black."

"I'll be back to try them one day soon."

"Bring Dylan. I'd love to see him. And watch out for McGuire."

McGuire's riding herd on him was the least of his worries. Taking it out on his son—on Helene's son—was a horse of a different color.

Troy had gone to prison because Glenn McGuire had twisted every speck of evidence against him. He would not get the chance to do that to Dylan.

If Troy had learned anything in prison, it was how to take care of business—by whatever means it took.

Chapter Seven

The blonde bitch hadn't died. Not that he'd meant to kill her originally, but since she'd fouled up everything for him, it would make him feel better to know she was no longer breathing.

Once again, he'd screwed things up. But there was no way he could have known the blonde would be there or that the guy in the black truck would show up.

He'd tracked Collette McGuire's every movement. She lived alone. She didn't date. No one had spent the night in that house except her for the past three months.

Ordinarily he could back off now, give things a chance to settle down, provide some damage control.

Not this time. Days, maybe hours, could make a difference.

Take one life to save another.

He'd killed for a lot less.

Chapter Eight

Dylan had balked at first, not wanting to start a war between her and her father, but Collette had persisted, and he'd finally agreed to let her stay at the ranch. His only stipulation had been that she tell her father beforehand.

She'd taken care of that a few seconds ago—after she'd asked how the investigation was going. There was no way she could have had a rational discussion with her father after telling him she was sleeping on murderer's row. His description, not hers.

Dylan turned into the drive that led to her house. Like most of the rural homes, this one sat well back from the road. Every other week, a neighbor kid cut the grass for her on his riding mower.

"Any word on fingerprints?" he asked Collette.

"The only matches were mine, yours and Eleanor's. I knew he had my and Eleanor's fingerprints on record. He made a point of getting them when we headed to Florida for spring break our freshman year at UT after telling us horror stories about women who were abducted by strangers. We figured it was to frighten us away from cute college guys we met on the beach."

"Did it work?"

"Until we met the first hunk. Did he take your fingerprints last night?"

"He did. It's routine, so don't go getting bent out of shape about it. Did your father say if they'd gotten any info from your wireless provider?"

"No, and I'm not sure he'll be able to get that information. When the stalker phones, my caller ID always indicates Out of Area or Unavailable. I think he uses prepaid phones."

"Even with those, you can get some information. The general location where the call originated. Whether or not he always used the same phone." Dylan killed the engine and opened the truck door. "Give me the name of your provider and I'll see what I can find out."

She told him and then jumped out of the truck and met him on the walkway that led to the front porch. "You're not a cop. How can you get info on my calls?"

"I have connections. My oldest brother, Wyatt, is a police detective in Atlanta."

"I see."

"That's one of the advantages of having five

brothers. You have a wide range of expertise to call on when you're in a jam."

"Are you close?"

"Not so close that I can tell you the name of Wyatt's current squeeze or what he ate for dinner last night, but close enough that I can ask a favor."

"When was the last time you saw Wyatt?"

"About four years ago when my grandmother died. All five of us were there for the funeral. The Ledger contingent was in full force that day."

Collette took the key from her handbag but didn't open the door. "How often do you all get together?"

"We tend to avoid reunions. When the five of us congregate, the topic of conversation tends to center around the things we all have in common. Mother's murder. Having a father in prison."

"But you're still family." Not that she had room to talk about failed family relationships. Collette unlocked the front door and pushed it open. The house felt cold and hostile, as if the aura of violence had attached itself to the very walls. It struck her that the Ledger home must feel a thousand times more frosty and intimidating to Dylan.

And she'd be sleeping in that same house tonight, with Dylan, his father and all their haunting memories of what used to be. She shuddered at the thought.

Dylan's hand came to rest on her shoulder. "Are you okay?"

"I will be when I get the house back in order. You can wait here if you like while I go change into work clothes."

"In that case, I think I'll make that call to Wyatt."

DYLAN PUNCHED IN WYATT'S cell-phone number. He had all his brothers' phone numbers programmed into his phone, though he seldom called them.

"You're on." Wyatt answered with his typical offbeat greeting.

"It's Dylan. Did I catch you at a bad time?"

"It's always a bad time around here. What's up? Problems in paradise already?"

"A few."

"Is Troy all right?"

It was never Dad with Wyatt.

"About what you'd expect."

"I have no idea what I'd expect."

"Dad's home. Quiet. Withdrawn, but talking about getting the ranch up and running again."

"Interesting. How are things working out for you?"

"They could be better."

"So, what's the problem?"

"I need some information."

"Sure. Can you hold on a minute?"

Dylan waited while Wyatt held a hurried conversation with someone else. There was loud talking in the background.

"Sorry," Wyatt said when he came back to Dylan. "I'm at the precinct. It's crazy around here."

"I won't keep you but a minute. I was wondering if you could get me the details on calls made from one cell phone to another in the Mustang Run area."

"Is some idiot harassing Troy already?"

"No. It's for a friend of mine. I'm guessing she could get the data herself but I figure you can get it a lot faster."

"A woman, huh? You're a fast worker."

"It's my killer charm."

"Must run in the family. So what's going on with her?"

"Her house was broken into last night and a girlfriend of hers who was there alone was attacked. Some guy's been making anonymous, harassing phone calls to my friend and she thinks he could be behind the assault."

"How serious were the victim's injuries?"

"He stabbed her in the shoulder with a kitchen knife. There was considerable blood loss and the wound required surgery. He also hit her in the head with a skillet. She suffered a concussion, but no major complications to this point."

"Sounds as if she was fighting him off and he missed his mark with the knife, or else he didn't mean to kill her. Either way, he's dangerous. The police should be handling this."

"They are."

"And you should be staying far away from this situation, Dylan. The Ledger name alone could make any attempt to help backfire on you."

Wyatt didn't know the half of it. "Can you get the info?"

"I'll need your friend's name, cell-phone number and her wireless provider."

Dylan obliged him, giving the name last.

"McGuire," Wyatt repeated. "Any kin to Sheriff Glenn McGuire?"

"His daughter."

"How in hell did you... Hold on a second, will you?"

This time Wyatt was back on the line in a matter of seconds.

"Things are hopping. Gotta run, but I'll get back to you. In the meantime, my advice is to run from this like you've got a couple of wild hogs chasing you."

"I'll keep that in mind. Thanks, bro."

Thanks for reiterating what he already knew.

Being with Collette was a mistake. Having her stay at his place against her dad's wishes was downright masochistic.

Dylan didn't see Collette when he walked through the house, but he could hear noises and music with a Latin beat coming from her bedroom. He stepped into the kitchen. The blood was still on the floor along with the mess the investigation team had made searching for evidence.

Dylan knew little about working a crime scene, but he figured they'd surely taken DNA samples. They'd also have taken the bloodied knife and skillet. Hopefully some concrete evidence would come of it. And Wyatt was right. They didn't need Dylan's help.

Still, he walked to the back door to check the lock. It was evident that it had been tampered with. His guess was that the man had come in and left that way. Dylan's first instinct about seeing a figure run from the house was probably right on target. He'd mentioned that to the sheriff during the interrogation session, but he had no idea if the sheriff had checked it out.

Dylan walked out the back door, across the porch and down the steps. The grass was high, probably due to be cut soon. There was no sign of footprints.

He scanned the area, looking for a protected spot where the attacker could have parked his car hidden from the road. There was a cluster of oak trees about fifty yards behind the house, but there were no tire tracks leading in that direction. If he'd parked there, he hadn't gotten there from Collette's driveway.

Dylan made his way to the trees, though he wouldn't wander far. Not that he expected trouble today. The attacker would have to be insane to chance coming back to the scene of the crime with Dylan's truck parked in the drive—the same truck that had most likely frightened him away last night.

The grass gave way to bare earth as Dylan reached the heavily shaded area. He knelt for a closer look at what appeared to be prints of rubber-soled shoes. The prints weren't totally distinct, but there was enough there to tell that the man had walked this way toward the house and then run back to his car. He held his foot next to one of the prints. He'd guess the attacker's shoe size at an eleven.

And just beyond the trees, there were well-indented tire tracks. He followed them just far enough to determine that the driver had cut across from a partially overgrown dirt road that ran behind the Baptist Church. The stalker had done his homework.

But he'd likely made a few mistakes. He'd have assumed Collette's car was parked in the garage, would have seen the shadows behind the blinds and mistook them for Collette's. And then Eleanor had surprised him, and he'd panicked and attacked her.

Had it been Collette alone inside the house...

Sick possibilities wreaked havoc with his mind.

Had the stalker come as he'd promised to convince Collette he was her soul mate? Or had he come to claim her against her will?

He'd love the stalker to show up now. Love to slam a fist into his face over and over until the man was mush.

He didn't know how he'd become this attached to Collette so quickly. All he knew was that he had to keep her safe.

Collette was on her knees in the kitchen when he returned to the house, scrubbing the blood stains with a terrycloth rag. The harsh odor of chemicals in the cleanser clogged his nostrils.

"Do you mind opening another window?" she asked without looking up.

He opened several and left the back door ajar.

"Thanks." Her yellow rubber gloves made a crinkling sound as she dipped the rag in the bucket of water and squeezed out the excess.

He watched her work, mesmerized by the movement of her body in the denim cutoffs and the soft pink T-shirt she'd changed into. She had a natural way about her that made her far more enticing than any glamour queen he'd ever seen. She was sensual without trying, feminine yet feisty and independent.

And what she did for a pair of denim cutoffs and a cotton shirt was affecting him in ways he didn't need right now. He had to find something to do besides stare at her derriere.

"Why don't you let me work on those stains while you go get your things together," he said.

"About that…" She dropped her rag into the bucket of soapy water and pulled off the gloves, dropping them onto the floor. "I've given that more thought. I can't intrude on you and your father when he's trying to adjust to life outside of prison and you're trying to reconnect with him. It wouldn't be fair to either of you."

He reached for her hand and pulled her to her feet. "Fine. Then I'll stay here with you."

"I can't ask you to do that."

"You didn't ask. I'm offering."

"And I'm turning you down. I have to move back into this house sooner or later."

"I'm not leaving you alone, Collette. Your place or mine. They're the only options, unless you want me to rent a hotel room for both of us."

"You're not making this easy, Dylan."

"It sounds easy enough to me."

"I can't take you away from your father. He needs you, probably even more than I do."

"Then it's settled. Get your things. You and your vivacious energy are probably exactly what the Ledger house needs." A new thought occurred to him. "Unless you're afraid my father is dangerous or that the house is haunted."

"From what I read in the newspaper yesterday, your father is exceptionally nonviolent. And I'd take ghosts over real live villains any day."

"Then it's settled. You pack. I'll clean."

"Forget about the scrubbing. I think I'll take my sister-in-law up on her offer to send her housekeeper my way for a day."

"Good. I hate scrub-pail hands."

He mussed her hair as if she were a kid, letting his fingers delve into the thick richness of it. "This should be fun. I haven't had a sleepover in years."

"A houseguest," she corrected him. "Sleeping in separate bedrooms."

He smiled. "Of course. Just a slip of the tongue."

He was far too smart to share a bed with Collette. He'd be out of here in a week or two, and she was going to be hell to get over as it was. Not that he had any idea where he was going. He only knew he couldn't go back to being cooped up in an office.

IF SOMEONE HAD TOLD Collette yesterday that she'd be staying over at Troy Ledger's house tonight, she'd have thought them daft. Dylan made the difference. They were still virtual strangers, yet she'd connected with him in a way that defied the odds.

Her heart had jumped to her throat when she'd accidentally caught him in the viewfinder yesterday, and being around him didn't lessen the impact. But if the attraction were purely physical, she'd have put him on the back burner while she dealt with her stalker and his attack on Eleanor.

But Dylan was protective without being patronizing. He hadn't lectured her about dealing with the stalker on her own or even hinted that this could be her fault.

And he'd discovered the footprints and tire tracks behind her house. She assumed her father had as well, but, of course, he wouldn't bother to mention any of that to her. Now all they needed was a good description of the rat from Eleanor.

"Do you mind driving to the hospital before we go back to the ranch?"

"Not at all. If Eleanor's talking, she could provide a lot of missing details."

"Maybe I should call first. If she can't have visitors yet, there's no reason to waste time on the drive."

She retrieved her cell phone and punched in the number for Eleanor's private room. She immediately recognized the voice that answered. "Good morning, Mrs. Baker. This is Collette."

"I'm glad you called. I was so stressed last night I don't know if I thanked you for staying with Eleanor until I could drive over from Houston."

"I was glad to do it, though Eleanor never knew I was there."

"Your father has already been in this morning. I'd heard a lot about him from Eleanor but had never met him. I feel a lot better after talking to him. He assured me he'll get to the bottom of this and arrest the thug who tried to kill Eleanor."

"I'm sure he will," Collette agreed. "How is Eleanor?"

"The doctor said the shoulder surgery went well. He doesn't expect any complications. I'm just glad you found her and got her to the hospital as quickly as you did."

"Actually, Dylan called for the ambulance even before I got home."

"Dylan?"

So her dad had failed to mention him. She'd love to know the reason for that. Likely more of his diabolical plan to put Dylan on the hot seat and keep Collette from trusting him.

"Dylan's a friend of mine and he arrived at the

house just before I did. It's possible the attacker ran from the scene when he heard Dylan drive up."

"Oh, my. I didn't know. Please thank him for me, as well."

"Is Eleanor up to having visitors? I'd love to stop by for a minute and say hello."

"I think it best if you wait. She's taking pain medication and the doctor wants her to get as much rest as possible. I wasn't in the room when the sheriff tried to question her, but he said she was still too groggy to respond coherently."

"Then she wasn't able to describe her attacker?"

"I'm not sure she even knows she was attacked. She keeps asking what happened to her."

"I understand. Please tell her that I called."

"I'll be sure to."

They said their goodbyes, and Collette broke the connection just as another call rang in.

"My dad," she announced to Dylan, "hopefully with news that he's made an arrest."

"Or at least identified a suspect other than me," he replied.

"Hi, Dad." She tried to keep her voice amicable even though she doubted he'd do the same. He didn't disappoint her.

"Have you come to your senses yet or are you still chasing after Dylan Ledger?"

"I'm with Dylan."

"You're putting yourself in danger for a man you know nothing about."

"Is that what you called to tell me?"

"No, I called to tell you that when I mentioned Dylan's name to Eleanor Baker, she became agitated and looked fearful."

"That's odd. I heard she was too groggy to talk to you. Dylan didn't attack her, Dad. The man who did left his footprints and the imprint of his tires behind my house. Dylan's truck was parked in the driveway."

"I suppose Dylan pointed those tracks out to you."

"Does it matter?" Collette said. "Just check them out and see for yourself."

The silence lasted too long.

"You already knew about the tracks, didn't you?"

"My deputies found them this morning after daylight, which would have given Dylan plenty of time to put them there himself to throw us off."

Unbelievable. "Do you really think Dylan is a suspect, or is all this just to keep me away from a Ledger?"

"You don't want to get mixed up with the likes of him."

Which pretty much answered her question. Anything she said at this point would only make matters worse. The barriers that separated them had grown almost impenetrable.

"Find my stalker, Dad. When you do, you'll have the man who attacked Eleanor."

"I'll find your stalker. Make no mistake about that. Your wireless provider was more than willing to work with us. I should know the second the pervert calls you—if he calls again."

"I'm glad to hear that."

"If you hear from him, act as if nothing has changed and keep him on the phone as long as possible. As soon as we get a lock on his location, I'll send the closest deputy to arrest him, hopefully even before he breaks the connection."

"Then you agree the stalker is the major suspect in this case?"

"He's a suspect. I haven't ruled out anyone as yet. I shouldn't need to remind you that your friend Eleanor's articles have made her more than a few enemies."

This was going nowhere. She shifted and moved the phone to her other ear. "Is there anything else I should know about the case?"

"Just that you're trusting the wrong man with your safety."

Her head began to pound at both temples. Why did everything with her father have to be so difficult? Resentment swelled inside her, not so much for the present as for the past.

If he'd ever been attuned to anyone's feelings but his own, her mother would still be alive.

DYLAN DODGED A LARGE turtle making its way across the road leading to the ranch house while Collette adjusted her visor to block the worst of the early afternoon rays. "I still think you should have given your father some advance warning that you're bringing the enemy home with you."

His lips cracked into an incredibly seductive smile that reached all the way to his mesmerizing eyes. "You're not the enemy."

"I doubt your father will see it that way."

"What could he possibly have against you?"

"How about the fact that Sheriff Glenn McGuire is determined to make you a suspect in a felony for no other reason than you're my friend?"

"It could be that your father is just doing his job."

"Are you always so generous in your opinions of people?"

"I'm not generous. I give people the benefit of the doubt. Until they prove me wrong."

Which made sense considering that was exactly what he was doing with his own father. Dylan was giving Troy Ledger a chance to be the father he hadn't been in eighteen years.

The circumstances of Troy Ledger's release

on a technicality had been covered ad nauseam in the local media, but she'd ignored most of it. That left her a little fuzzy on the details. As she understood it, the reversal involved some supposedly coerced testimony. The prosecutor at the time had since retired and moved to a Caribbean island, so she doubted they'd ever get the full story.

Nonetheless, some, like her father, would always see Troy Ledger as guilty and hold that against Dylan, as well. Others, like the cute young waitress at Abby's Diner, obviously couldn't care less.

She'd flirted with him shamelessly when they'd stopped there for lunch before driving to the ranch. And Abby herself had seemed genuinely happy to see Dylan. She hadn't even let them pay for their meals.

Abby had claimed it was worth it seeing the way Dylan appreciated her food. More than appreciated, he'd devoured the noonday special of chicken-fried steak smothered in cream gravy with mashed potatoes, pinto beans and corn bread on the side. He'd topped that off with Abby's famous coconut pie.

Collette had choked down half a burger and a tall glass of iced tea. It churned in her stomach as Dylan stopped his truck in front of the Ledger ranch house. To her surprise, what looked to be an almost-new horse trailer was parked in the driveway.

Looking past that, she spotted a tall but muscular man standing on the front porch, nonchalantly leaning against a support post and peeling an orange. His hair was the same dusty brown color as Dylan's but without the sun streaks that gave Dylan the appearance of a real cowboy. The man's lips looked as if they'd been pulled tight for so long that a smile might crack them.

"I'm not sure what the horse trailer's about," Dylan said as he jumped out and grabbed her bag from the backseat of the double-cab pickup.

"Your father may have bought some horses."

"Anything's possible." He sounded doubtful.

Collette stepped from the truck and into a muddy patch where a water hose had recently run, likely to water the horses. Thankfully, she'd taken a quick shower after her scrubbing routine and changed into a pair of black slacks and a pair of Western work boots. She'd even tamed the wildest locks of her thick red hair.

Troy stared at her as if she were trespassing on sacred ground. A deacon at their church, a man she'd known all her life, stepped from the house just as she and Dylan reached the porch. She considered his appearance a reprieve as she sucked in a gulp of fresh air.

"Well, look who's here," Bob said in his

booming voice. "Collette. And you must be Dylan." He stuck out a hand in Dylan's direction. "Bob Adkins. If I have my Ledger brothers straight, the last time I saw you, you were claiming bragging rights about a catfish that got away."

Dylan set her bag down on the porch. "I hate to say that I don't remember you, but nice to meet you."

"Wouldn't expect you to remember me. Good to have you back in Mustang Run. Good to have your father back, too."

Collette was relieved that Bob had come over to welcome Troy Ledger home. He was one of the most respected men in town, and his acceptance would go a long way. Even the hard-nosed sheriff would not attempt to tell Bob whom he could befriend.

"Bob brought over a couple of horses," Troy said.

"Yep." Bob grinned and nodded. "I thought you could use them to ride your land and see what kind of shape the outbuildings, pastures and fences are in. Keep the young fillies as long as you need. They need to be ridden anyhow. The roan's Lady, the chestnut is Ginger. If I forgot any tack that you need, give me a holler."

"Great," Dylan said. "I can't wait to give them a workout."

Bob turned his attention to Collette. "I heard you had some trouble at your place last night."

"Someone broke in and attacked my friend. That's why I'm here with Dylan. He's volunteered for bodyguard service until the perpetrator is apprehended."

"Good idea. Any guy who earned a silver star in Iraq passes muster in my book."

That was more information she didn't know about Dylan, and she wondered how Bob did.

"I'd love to chew the fat a little longer," Bob continued, "but I'd best get back to the ranch. By the way, Ruby Nelle told me to tell the both of you that she wants to have you over for dinner as soon as you get settled in."

Troy set his half-eaten orange on the porch railing and wiped his hands on his jeans before stepping to the edge of the porch with Bob. "Thanks," he said. "Your friendship means a lot. Ruby Nelle's, too."

"Think nothing of it. We go way back, Troy. Long as I got a biscuit, you got half."

They waited on the porch until Bob drove away, pulling the horse trailer behind him.

"Collette's going to be staying with us for a few days," Dylan said.

"I kind of figured that, what with you carrying a bag."

"Unless it's a problem," Collette added quickly.

Troy's expression stayed fixed into the grim stare. "Might be a problem for the sheriff."

"I'm an adult. My father doesn't make my decisions."

Troy shrugged. "Then you're welcome to stay. Place isn't much to brag about. Bare necessities, that's about it."

"I'm sure it's fine."

To Collette's surprise, Troy picked up her overnight bag. "I'll show you to the guest room so you can put your things away."

She followed Troy down the hall to an extension that jutted off the back of the house. The bedroom was at the end of that short hallway. A queen-size mahogany four-poster covered in a blue-and-white quilt dwarfed the cozy area and matched the antique dresser. Beside the bed was a large hook rug, worn but spotlessly clean.

On the far wall, double windows opened to the remains of a long-neglected English garden that fit between this and a matching extension off the other side of the house, providing a sunlit area protected from the wind.

Vines climbed over odd-shaped rocks and around flowerbeds that were overgrown with weeds. A few lone daffodils had fought their way through the dense foliage. A stone wall at the back of the garden made the area seem totally private, yet open to the heavens.

Collette stared in awe. "What a terrific spot for a garden."

"Helene designed it and the extensions to the house. Our bedroom was in the opposite extension so that the garden could be the first thing she saw when she woke in the morning. As overworked as she was caring for five boys, she spent hours tending those flowers."

Sadness sank so deep into his voice that Collette had to swallow hard to fight back tears.

"Guess it's not that great a view now." With that, Troy turned and strode away, leaving her alone to stare at Helene's forsaken oasis.

The stories of ghosts haunting the house crept into her mind. Maybe the ghost of Helene Ledger did still live inside these walls, waiting all these years for Troy and her boys to come home.

The piercing ring of Collette's cell phone startled her back to reality. She checked the caller ID. Unavailable.

Chills froze her breath and stilled her heart. As always, the living were far more frightening to her than the dead.

Chapter Nine

"I'm glad you answered, my sweet. I've been worried about you."

Collette's stomach turned at the term of endearment, but she had to play this cool. "Why would you be worried about me?"

"I heard that someone broke into your house and attacked your guest. You should use more care in choosing your friends."

"What is that supposed to mean?"

"Your friend obviously has enemies. Everyone adores you—as I do."

He was playing this to the hilt, further proof of how vicious and callous he was.

"You know nothing about me."

"Ah, but I do. I know and love everything about you. Even your scent intoxicates me. It's Cartier, isn't it?"

Her stomach swirled in nauseous waves. Had he been that close to her without her knowing it? Or had he been inside her house before last night, touched her things, or done God only knew what else?

"Either tell me who you are, or get out of my life."

"I'm only trying to comfort you and keep you safe. Hanging out with Dylan Ledger is not helping with that."

She stared out the window, imagining him somewhere beyond the stone wall that bordered the old garden. Her senses teemed with urgency, as if he might appear in the flesh at any second.

She should never have come here, never have pulled Dylan and his father into her entanglements with a madman.

"I must go now. Keep safe, my love, until we talk again." Then the line went dead.

The conversation had been short, as always. He might have suspected from the first that his location was being traced. She punched in her father's cell number. When there was no answer, she left a message.

Just because the sheriff hadn't answered didn't mean a deputy wasn't already aware of the stalker's call. If the monster was on or near Willow Creek Ranch, deputies could be speeding this way even now. She should alert Dylan and Troy.

Before she could, there was a tap at the open bedroom door.

"Come in."

Dylan stepped inside just as her father returned her call. "Give me a moment," she said. "I have to take this."

Dylan nodded and stepped closer. His presence wrapped around her even though they weren't touching. There was no ignoring his rugged virility, but it was the calm, understated support he gave so naturally that she needed most right now.

Never one to mince words, her father jumped in as soon as she'd answered. "We've got the general location he was calling from."

"It's Willow Creek Ranch, isn't it?"

"Not even close."

She exhaled sharply in pure relief. "So where is he?"

The answer shot a new surge of terror straight to her heart.

DYLAN WATCHED Collette's guard come crumbling down as she tossed her phone on the bed. He reached for her and pulled her into his arms. He tensed when her face burrowed into his chest. He was overstepping the boundaries of their tenuous relationship.

But she didn't pull away, and he didn't want to

let her go. He liked the feel of her in his arms, liked the fragrance of her hair and the sensation of the curling locks beneath his chin.

"I take it that was bad news," he said, once she'd gathered her resolve and pulled away.

"My stalker called again."

That confused him. "I assumed from the conversation that you were talking to your father."

"I was then, but that was the second call. Dad called to say that they'd tracked the stalker's call."

"Wouldn't that be a good thing?"

"The stalker is somewhere inside Carlton-Hayes Regional Hospital."

He muttered a low curse. No wonder Collette had taken an emotional dive. The brutal rat was now stalking Eleanor as well, walking the halls of the hospital where she was recovering from his almost-deadly assault.

"What does your father plan to do?"

"The hospital is out of his jurisdiction, but he can have the local police chief provide round-the-clock guards for her room, at least for the time being." She wrapped her fingers around the bedpost. "The perverted brute must know that Eleanor can identify him and he plans to kill her before she can."

That seemed the most logical conclusion, except that if he'd attacked Eleanor when she surprised him in the house, why not finish her off last night?

Still, he hated to see Collette so upset. Dylan took both her hands in his. "It sounds as if your father has the situation under control. I'm sure they're not going to let this guy into Eleanor's hospital room, and she's not going anywhere. She'll be safe."

"I wish I felt as sure as you sound."

So did Dylan. "What do you say we go take a look at the horses? Better yet, we could take a ride and see if I can still find that old swimming hole."

"Tired of hearing me whine?"

He squeezed her hands. "Tired of seeing you look as if the world just came crashing down on top of you."

She nodded. "Give me a minute to lather on some sunscreen. I burn at the mention of sunshine."

"Take your time. I'll be in the kitchen—unless you need help with the sunscreen," he teased.

He was rewarded with the first real smile he'd seen on her gorgeous lips. But that was only because she didn't realize how much he'd actually enjoy rubbing in the lotion.

He found his father in the kitchen, staring out the window the way he seemed to spend half his time. Dylan wondered what went on in his mind during those zombielike sessions. Whatever it was, the thoughts planted a haggard look on his father's face and sucked the life from his somber eyes.

"I guess I should have called you before I brought Collette home with me." Home. The word sounded strange on his tongue yet it had slipped out effortlessly.

Troy stepped away from the window and leaned against the counter. "No need. It's your house, too, long as you want to stay."

"Thanks."

"I'm more concerned about what's going on between you and Collette," Troy said.

"I told you. She needs protection. I've got nothing better to do."

"And her being single and gorgeous has nothing to do with it?"

"Makes the job more pleasant."

"Just watch yourself, Dylan. The sheriff will make trouble for you eight ways to Sunday if he thinks there's anything going on between you two. I'm not saying she wouldn't be worth it. I'm just warning you."

"I barely know her."

"Love doesn't always wait for that. I knew from the first day I met your mother that there would never be anyone else for me." He worried the scar on his face with his right hand. "There never was."

Ever since the murder, Dylan had been brainwashed by his grandparents, aunts and uncles to believe that his father had committed the brutal, despicable act. He'd never bought into it.

He was even more convinced of his father's innocence now. However, that didn't end the issues between them.

"Do you mind if Collette and I take the horses for a ride?"

"Bob brought them over to be ridden. Check out the condition of the ranch while you're at it. I'm looking to buy a starter herd of cattle next week. I can't hack this sitting around doing nothing. Even in prison, we kept busy. If we hadn't, I'd have gone insane."

"Hard work won't hurt you," Dylan agreed.

"Guess you had plenty of that in the service. Eight years, wasn't it?"

Dylan nodded. Eight years, and he'd walked as close to death as a man could get and still come out in one piece. Never once had he heard from his father. Not then and not when Dylan was younger and had sent Troy countless letters and pictures. Photographs of Dylan playing varsity football, running track and swaggering around in his first pair of authentic Western boots since moving away from Willow Creek Ranch. He'd been sixteen at the time and had bought them with money from his first summer job.

A letter or a phone call from his dad back then would have meant the world to Dylan. Better late than never might not be enough to cut it at this stage in his life.

"I guess Bob Adkins told you about my time in the army when he stopped by today?"

"Yep. You turned into quite a man."

With no help from you.

The old anger and rejection kicked up inside Dylan, and he knew that if he didn't get out of this house right now, he'd explode.

"Tell Collette I'll be outside."

COLLETTE TOOK THE beautiful cinnamon-colored roan to a full gallop, loving the feel of the wind in her face and the warmth of the sun on her back. Her mother used to claim that spring in the hill country was like a rhapsody, the melody a perfect blending of scents, colors and sounds that made just breathing seem like a rebirth.

Collette couldn't claim rejuvenation in the midst of all her problems, but the ride through the rolling hills with new growth budding all around her had lulled her anxiety to a more wieldy level.

Dylan's mount was a flaxen chestnut, a bit more nervous than hers, but quite regal. Dylan had calmed her with a steady voice when approaching and saddling her, and the filly had quickly settled down. He clearly had the same knack for charming horses as he did her.

He had that deliciously laid-back cowboy way about him even when she knew coming home to face his father after all these years had to be stirring up an emotional storm inside him.

Dylan slowed the chestnut to a trot. He pointed to his left as she reined in her spirited mount so that she could ride beside him.

"That's the legendary Ledger swimming hole where my brothers and I used to escape our chores every chance we got."

"I can see why."

The vista was breath-stealing. Beautiful willows dotted the banks, and the clear blue water sparkled like dancing jewels in the bright sunlight. A silvery fish jumped in the middle of the pool creating a circle of widening ripples. A stately blue heron stood on the bank, looking so still and perfect it could have passed for a statue.

She brought the roan to a dead stop to watch a fawn that studied them from beneath the spreading branches of an oak tree on the other side of the pond. When Dylan slid from his saddle to the sea of grass, the animal turned and disappeared into a cluster of scrubby oaks, rough-leaf dogwoods and underbrush.

She pushed her sunglasses to the top of her head for a better look. "It's so peaceful out here."

"Which is not at all the way I remember it."

Lady pawed the ground, ready to be off again, but Dylan took the reins while Collette dismounted.

"It was never quiet back when my brothers and I were out here together. See that old rope hanging from the oak near where that deer was drinking before we startled it?"

"I see it."

"It's a bit gnarled and shredding now, but that was our version of a water park in the good old days."

The good old days, before brutal violence had stolen his youth. She hurt for that boy even though she marveled at the man he'd become. He led the horses to the edge of the water for a cooling drink after their vigorous run.

"Did you really earn a silver star in Iraq?"

"Can't say that I did, at least no more than anyone else who served there. I just happened to get noticed and they presented me with one."

"Methinks you're a bit too modest."

"No, just honest. You don't really think about your actions in the heat of battle. You just do what you're trained to do and try to keep yourself, your combat buddies and innocent civilians alive."

When the fillies had drunk their fill, he tied the reins to a low-hanging branch of one of the willows. That done, he proceeded to unbutton his long-sleeved blue Western shirt. Anticipation hummed through her senses as the shirt opened, revealing well-defined abs and a dusting of hairs on his tanned flesh.

He shrugged out of the shirt and spread it on top of the prickly blades of grass, then motioned for her to have a seat. Giddy with desire, she dropped to the shirt and pulled her knees up to her chest.

Stretching beside her, he propped himself up on his elbow to face her. The closeness was intimate, and the temptation to lie back and press her body against his was all but irresistible.

Dylan tugged on the brim of his Stetson, pulling it lower to block some of the sun's rays. Even then, stray locks of his dusty brown hair escaped to fall over his forehead.

"Tell me about Eleanor," he said.

The statement cooled the desire she'd almost succumbed to and brought the real reason for their being together back into sharp focus.

"I told you all I know. We've been friends since college. She's a go-getter investigative reporter who also likes to have fun. And she and Melinda are fascinated with the ghosts and spirits. That's probably the one thing I don't have in common with them."

"Investigative reporting can gain a person lots of enemies."

"No doubt it does, but what got her attacked was showing up at my house on the wrong night."

"Still, I'd like to know more about her and any enemies she might have."

"The stalker was harassing me, and he called from the hospital where she's recovering. Isn't that proof that Eleanor is just a victim of circumstance?"

"It would seem that way, but when you're sure the enemy is dead ahead and things are under control, you'd best watch your back."

"Meaning you think there's more to this than the obvious?"

"I'm not saying that your analysis of the situation is wrong, Collette. I'd just like a better scope of the landscape. Do you have Internet access at your house?"

"Yes, but both my desktop and my laptop are at my studio. Why?"

"I'd like to research Eleanor's recent articles and determine which ones could be considered incendiary."

"Incendiary, as in the articles Dad decided made you a suspect. I don't think we should go down that road, Dylan."

"It won't hurt to check them out. Where's your studio?"

"In the old section of town. It's only a couple of blocks from Abby's Diner."

Thank goodness, he let the subject drop. Silence melded into a gentle truce, and when he reached over and trailed his fingers down her arm, her need for him became a shimmering heat of ribbon that corded around her heart.

"Tell me about yourself, Dylan."

"I'm overeducated, unemployed and unattached. I'm a steak-and-potato kind of guy who prefers beer to champagne and would rather be tied and flogged than stuffed into a suit and tie. I'd say that pretty much sums me up."

If so, he was much more than the sum of his parts. But it was the unattached part that intrigued her at the moment. "Have you ever been married?"

"No."

"Engaged?"

"No. I have had sex before, though. As best I remember, I liked it a lot."

As best she remembered, she hadn't been all that impressed with the act itself. She had an idea that conclusion wouldn't hold with Dylan. A burn crept to her cheeks, and she turned away to keep him from seeing it.

"What about you?" Dylan asked.

"I've never been married, but I was engaged once. It didn't work out. The fire died before the ink on the wedding invitations dried."

"His loss."

"It was a long time ago. I'm sure he's forgotten all about me."

"That's doubtful."

His fingers left her arm to climb the column of her neck and entangle in her hair. Her pulse spiked. How could she possibly react to his touch this way when her life and Eleanor Baker's were in a state of chaotic danger? Nonetheless, desire grew red-hot inside her. She stretched out beside Dylan, spread her hand over the bare hardness of his chest and pressed her lips against his.

He kissed her back, tentatively at first, but then ravenously, as if he couldn't get enough. She trembled in his arms as the hot, deep, slow kisses awakened a throbbing passion inside her.

His hands roamed from her neck and hair to her abdomen. His thumbs rode upward until they brushed the swell of her nipples, the movement arousing and titillating through the thin cotton of her shirt.

She knew if they didn't stop soon, they wouldn't stop at all. Her inhibitions kicked in, and calling on all the restraint she could rally, she pulled away.

He had to be a bit sexually frustrated at the abrupt halt, but still he managed a smile that sent her senses soaring again.

"Never had that much excitement at the swimming hole before," he teased.

"And with your boots on."

The flirtatious interplay was disrupted by the tones of Dylan's cell phone.

The delicious moment faded into oblivion as she watched his expression turn grim. Cold chills replaced the warmth in her veins and reality returned with a punishing vengeance.

Chapter Ten

"My gut feeling is that this is far more compli-cated than an overzealous stalker and that Col-lette McGuire is in imminent danger."

Wyatt's words couldn't have gotten to Dylan more if they'd been delivered by a fist to the gut. "Did you come to this conclusion just from checking her phone records?"

"That and past experience. I've dealt with this type of stalking behavior before."

"So you think we're dealing with a psycho nutcase?"

"No. I think you're dealing with a cagey, calculating male who knows exactly what he's doing."

"Were you able to identify the caller?"

"No. That's part of the problem. He used pre-paid cell phones that couldn't be traced and in some instances, he stole phones and made the calls before the owner discovered they were miss-ing and stopped the service. Your run-of-the-mill nonviolent stalker seldom goes to that extreme to remain anonymous."

"You said that was one of the problems. What are the others?"

"He made the calls from different places and at different times of the day so there's no way we can pinpoint his schedule. One was made from Willow Creek Ranch yesterday."

"Collette was inside the house with me when he made that one."

"I suspected as much. He's following her. I'm not convinced it's love or even lust that is motivating his actions."

"What motivators are you considering?"

"Jealousy. Revenge. Betrayal—or perceived betrayal. Those are the most common."

"Collette seems certain she doesn't know the caller."

"I'm just throwing out possibilities."

"What do you make of the most recent contact, the call made from the hospital where Eleanor Baker is being treated?"

"That must have occurred after I got the report. How did you learn about it?"

"Sheriff McGuire called Collette. He's convinced she's in danger, too. Of course, he thinks being with me is adding to her peril."

"Don't underestimate Glenn McGuire. As for the call from Eleanor's hospital, that definitely adds a new layer to the case. You need to be really careful, Dylan. Criminals don't follow rules of engagement."

"Neither did terrorists."

"Good point. Do you want me to fax you the data I collected?"

"You could, if I had access to a fax machine."

"I have one in my studio," Collette interrupted. She gave him the number, and he relayed it to Wyatt.

"One other thing," Wyatt said.

"Hit me with it."

"Are you totin'?"

"I have a Glock .45 in my truck's glove compartment. Wouldn't travel without it. And I have a rifle on the truck's gun rack. When in Rome… or in this case Texas."

"Keep them handy, but don't go trying to steal the sheriff's job. I can understand your trying to keep his daughter safe—well, actually I can't, but that's your business. Apprehending criminals is the sheriff's business."

"Got it."

"Good. Take care, bro, and keep me posted."

"Will do. Thanks."

Dylan broke the connection, already dreading going over this with Collette. Wyatt's info further complicated the ideas he'd already considered and added a couple of new alternatives to the mix.

Welcome to Texas.

THE COZY, USUALLY QUIET office in Collette's photography studio was a whirlwind of activity. The fax machine hummed as it spit out page after page of calls made to and from her cell phone over the past few months. Dylan's fingers tapped against the keyboard of her desktop. Water dripped through the grounds and into the Thermos belly of her automatic coffeemaker.

Against this backdrop of purposeful activity, Collette was reduced to doodling meaningless scribbles on the edge of the notes she'd made while talking to Eleanor's mother.

Eleanor was alert but had no memory of the attack. The last thing she remembered was walking into the kitchen to return her empty dinner plate. Temporary memory lapses after a concussion were not unusual occurrences, the medical staff had assured the family. In most instances the patient regained full or at least partial memory of the event causing the injury.

Bottom line, they couldn't be sure when or if she'd be able to describe her attacker. In the meantime, there was nothing to do on that front but wait.

Dylan was using her desktop computer to surf

the Net for articles written by Eleanor. Collette looked over his shoulder for a minute, then picked up her laptop and took it to the sitting area where she normally discussed prices and picture packages with clients.

Dropping to the most comfortable of the chairs, she turned on the computer and started to type in *Eleanor Baker,* changing her mind before she reached the second *e.* She changed the search criteria to *Troy Ledger's murder trial.* Hundreds of choices lined up on the screen.

She clicked on the most promising and started reading an account of the evidence presented against him during the course of the trial. She scanned one article after another. The mild irritation she experienced at first became a tightening in her chest and then a sickening surge of disbelief.

Troy Ledger had been sentenced to life in prison based on conjecture, circumstantial evidence and the testimony of his dead wife's parents, Collette's father and a few other locals.

In contrast, the defense had claimed that Sheriff McGuire never searched for the real killer once Troy Ledger had been confirmed as a suspect. The sole focus of her father's investigation was said to be collecting evidence to convict Troy, who had publicly criticized the sheriff's handling of a previous investigation involving two migrant workers accused of stealing from their employer.

Helene's parents had testified that Troy protested when they tried to give their daughter and their grandchildren money or nice gifts and trips, even though he couldn't provide them. Character witnesses for Troy had said that while he was stubborn and independent, he was a nonviolent man who loved his wife and kids and provided the necessities.

The conviction clinchers had been the fact that Helene was shot with Troy's pistol, coupled with his unwillingness to cooperate in his own defense and the testimony of one of Helene's best friends who said she'd stopped by the Willow Creek Ranch the morning of the murder and found Helene packing a bag. When she'd asked her where she was going, Helene had said to her parents', that she'd let things go on too long.

Troy Ledger had claimed his innocence, but for the most part, he'd seemed angry and sullen or else totally detached from the trial proceedings. When he'd finally taken the stand, he'd broken down and cried. One of the articles claimed that the jurors had apparently seen that remorse as guilt.

The family of the murdered wife had cheered at the conviction. Dylan and his brothers were not present for any of the proceedings except the sentencing.

Collette leaned back in the chair and studied Dylan's profile as she mentally reviewed the findings about his father. Deep in thought as he was, the tiny wrinkles that creased Dylan's eyes when he smiled were all but invisible. The muscles in his arms weren't flexed, but they still pushed at the fabric of his shirt. He was as tough and independent as his father must have been.

She wondered if Dylan would ever find out the truth about what had really gone on at Willow Creek Ranch the day his mother had been murdered. Unless Troy Ledger was innocent, she hoped he never did.

Knowing that your father had destroyed your mother was a cross she'd never wish on anyone.

Exhausted, she leaned back and stared at the clock on the wall opposite her. It was half past nine in the evening, and she'd gotten very little sleep last night. No wonder she was fading. She closed her eyes, but now it was her own mother's tragic death that weighed heavy on her mind.

"I CAN'T BELIEVE you hired an attorney after I told you I didn't want one."

Dylan spoke through clenched teeth, determined to keep his voice low enough that Collette would not hear the argument from wherever she'd disappeared to in the house. She'd escaped the table and the tension right after Troy had announced that he'd hired an attorney to represent Dylan before the sheriff came up with an arrest warrant.

Troy held a bowl beneath the faucet and rinsed away remains of the beef stew he'd cooked for dinner. "You'd think differently if you knew the sheriff the way I do."

"There is no evidence against me."

"I told you this morning. The evidence is whatever Glenn McGuire says it is. Believe me. I know."

"This isn't about you. It's not even about me. It's about stopping a lunatic before he kills someone."

"And if he does, you'll find yourself behind bars so fast, you won't even have time to think about what happened. And she'll be dead. That's all you'll know."

His father's hands began to shake, and the glass he'd just picked up slipped from his soapy fingers and hit the floor, sending slivers of glass in every direction.

Seeing his father like this stole the thunder from Dylan's anger and resentment. His release from prison would have been traumatic enough without being hurled back into his past by an assault that had nothing to do with him.

Drops of blood dripped from Troy's thumb as he cleaned up the broken glass with his bare hands. Dylan handed him a paper towel and tried to think of something to say to a man who had become a virtual stranger to him. Too many years had passed. Too much had gone unsaid.

"I wish we'd have connected sooner," Dylan said.

"Now's a fine time to think about that." Troy picked up the towel, brushed tiny shards of glass from his hand and walked away.

The last words had sounded like an accusation. The irony of that set Dylan on edge. Never had a kid needed a father more than he had. But he didn't pursue it.

"I noticed first-aid supplies in the hall bathroom," he said instead. "Take care of the cut. I'll finish up here."

"The cut's nothing."

Fine by him. Dylan walked away and went in search of Collette, though he hoped she'd gone to bed. She'd dozed in the chair back at her office, but she needed more than a catnap after what she'd been through.

Instead he found her on the front porch, sitting on the top step, her gorgeous hair tousled by the wind, her face tinged with moonlight.

His muscles grew relaxed. His need for her grew heady. Two days and he'd already fallen harder for her than he'd ever fallen for anyone. The situation probably had something to do with his letting himself get so close so quickly. But it was Collette who made it feel so right.

"Sorry to bring you into that father/son moment."

"No need to apologize. I just thought you needed a little privacy."

Dylan sat on the steps beside her. "I actually think he means well, but he can't separate this from what happened to him."

"Can you blame him? I mean if he's innocent, then he was wrongly convicted. It's only natural he'd worry that the same could happen to you. He lost eighteen years of his life."

"Seventeen," Dylan corrected, though it didn't make much difference.

"Eighteen," Collette repeated. "The year he spent waiting for the trial must have been the most horrific of all. He'd lost his wife to violence and his kids to a family that hated him."

"You're right. I came here to see if there was a way we could forge a bond, but on some level, I think I'm trying to start a fight."

"Forging bonds takes time." She leaned back against the porch railing and faced him. "My being here doesn't help."

"It helps me," he said. "At least when you're here I know you're safe." He reached for her hand.

He liked how it felt in his and knew it wouldn't take much for him to lose control with her. A few kisses like they'd shared this afternoon, and his hunger for her would explode like a grenade.

They sat without talking for five minutes or more while the night wrapped around them. The hum of crickets and the high-pitched chirping of tree frogs created a soothing backdrop for the fireflies that darted among a patch of povertyweed.

Dylan stretched and leaned against the post at the top of the steps. "I don't remember it ever being this quiet. Mom used to say we kids made enough racket to raise the dead. Dad always countered that it's when we were quiet that he worried."

Odd how that came back to him now when he hadn't thought of it in years. Back then he hadn't had a care in the world. If his parents had, they'd hidden it well. He'd heard them argue, but not that often. Instead, they'd laughed a lot. On nights like this, they'd held hands in the porch swing while he and his brothers had played chase or wrestled in the grass.

Collette scooted closer. "I always envied my friends who had large, boisterous families."

"How many siblings do you have?"

"Just my brother, Bill, and we were never that

close. He's too much like my father for us to get along."

"Is he in law enforcement, too?"

"No. He has an insurance agency, but he's adopted my father's opinionated and domineering ways."

"You must have taken after your mother. I know you look a lot like she did."

"Unfortunately, that's the only way we're alike. Mom was patient and far too submissive for her own good. I may have inherited just a streak of my father's stubbornness."

"You?" he teased.

"A tiny streak."

"What happened to your mother?" he asked. "And feel free to tell me it's none of my business if you don't want to talk about it."

"She had an accident. After that she had several strokes before her body just shut down."

"I'm sorry."

"So am I."

Collette seemed to pull inside herself, and Dylan slipped an arm around her shoulder. "How long has it been?"

"She died the week I graduated from UT. I gave up the position I had waiting for me in D.C. I needed time to get over the grief. By the time I did, I realized I liked the flexibility of owning and operating my photography business and living here in Mustang Run."

"You must miss her a lot."

"I do." She stretched and massaged the back of her neck. "I'm really tired. I think I'll call it a night."

"Good idea. It's almost midnight."

He stood and tugged her to her feet as headlights from an approaching vehicle bounced off the trees and shot rays of illumination across the terrain. Dylan jumped up and raced to his truck for his rifle. Before he reached it, a sleek sports car sped into view.

"My brother," Collette announced, "no doubt here to deliver a new set of orders from on high."

Dylan left the gun in the truck. He offered a hand when Bill started up the walk. Bill ignored it and walked right past him. Dylan resisted the temptation to teach him a few manners in a way that would have Bill McGuire rolling on the ground in pain. It wouldn't be a fair fight. Bill's muscles looked as if the heaviest thing he'd lifted in years was his briefcase.

Collette stood her ground at the top of the steps, her shoulders back and her hands propped on her slender hips. "I suppose Dad sent you."

"It doesn't matter who sent me. Coming out

here is totally irresponsible. Get your things and get in the car."

"I'm not going with you, and you owe Dylan Ledger an apology for barging in here like a mad bull."

"Dylan had no business bringing you to his ranch. Surely you didn't expect us to sit by while you shack up with the son of a murderer."

Dylan's blood began to boil. "If you have concerns about Collette being out here, that's fine. But don't act like she's doing anything inappropriate. Got it?"

That's when the twerp made a big mistake. He shoved Dylan.

Dylan grabbed Bill's arm and felt his fingers dig into the man's flabby bicep.

Collette stamped her foot and inserted herself between them. "Would you both please just stop this? I don't need rescuing or defending. I'm capable of deciding where I want to be and, yes, Bill, even whom I want to shack up with if I so choose."

Dylan exhaled sharply and let go of Bill's arm. Pulverizing Collette's brother wouldn't help the situation. Even letting the guy know that he could would serve little purpose except to vent his own anger.

"Go home, Bill," Collette ordered. "If Dad has anything to say to me, he knows where I am."

"This isn't like your usual fights with Dad, Collette. This time your obstinacy could get you killed."

"It's my life. I'll take that chance."

"Fine. I'm washing my hands of the situation." Bill glared at Dylan, then turned and stormed to his car without looking back.

Dylan reached over and pushed a wild lock of red curls from Collette's face, tucking it behind her ear. "Are you sure? I'd worry about you but I'd understand if you wanted to go with him."

"I'm sure, Dylan. I'm not going anywhere without you."

Her eyes locked with his, and the desire to keep her safe melded with a need so earthy and primal that he felt it inside every cell of his body.

He'd never wanted a woman more.

Which meant he'd best not stand here staring into her bewitching eyes another second.

He fit a hand to the small of her back. "Let's go inside. It's been a long day and we both could use some rest."

But it wasn't rest he was craving when he followed her inside and down the hallway to her room.

DEEP PURPLE SHADOWS merged into bizarre shapes that danced eerily across the ceiling. Collette stared at them, enthralled by the shifting patterns. She'd fallen asleep immediately only to wake again before dawn. Her eyes were heavy, her mind captured in that state of drowsy confusion, somewhere between sleep and wakefulness.

Slivers of moonlight filtered through the curtains at the window painting shimmering strings of light across the blue coverlet. Collette closed her eyes only to open them again when a frigid chill infiltrated the room. She shivered and pulled the quilt to her neck, but the frost was bone deep.

A figure coalesced, dressed in a white gown with tattered remnants that swirled about the room as if they had wings of their own. Collette watched, mesmerized, rapt by the essence of the ghostly image.

Fear suffused her senses, but she couldn't bring herself to try to escape or even to look away.

"Are you Helene Ledger?" she asked, unsure if she was whispering the words or if they were being pulled from her mind by the ghostly vision.

"Get out of my house," the apparition ordered.

Frosty swirls drifted from the figure and from Collette's breath. The chill was real. So was the ghost.

"Why should I leave?"

"You bring danger to yourself and to my boy."

The figure grew translucent, and the swirls of white disconnected for a few seconds, then reunited again on the other side of the room.

"I would never hurt Dylan. But he's not a little boy, Helene. He's a man, a very brave man, and he's trying to help me."

"Leave my house. Go to your father. He's the one who brought the trouble on you. He will destroy my family."

The words echoed in Collette's mind, but if the spirit haunting her was Helene, why would she appear to Collette instead of to Troy or Dylan?

"You must leave this house, but be very, very careful. Death is bearing down on you."

But death wasn't talking. The ghost was. "Did your husband kill you, Helene? Is that why you're trapped in this house?"

"Go, before you bring danger to the ones I love."

The tiers of white snapped as if they'd been cracked like a whip. A second later the spirit vanished, and the room grew so hot, Collette was afraid it might burst into flame.

She jumped out of bed and tore off her pajamas. But the temperature changed again, leaving the room chilly but not frigid. She grabbed the emerald-colored cashmere robe she'd brought with her and pulled it tight around her naked body.

A nightmare, though she hadn't realized she'd drifted off to sleep.

That's all it could have been. A frightening reaction to all that had happened over the past two days.

Just a vivid dream. Yet even now it seemed infinitely more real than the present. Helene's words obsessed her, playing over and over like a mantra.

He's the one who brought the trouble on you. He will destroy my family.

Collette's father couldn't be responsible for her stalker, but he could have been behind Troy Ledger's arrest and conviction.

Now he was nursing a grudge against Dylan that would grow stronger as long as she stayed at Willow Creek Ranch.

Perhaps she should call Bill to come back for her first thing in the morning, before she actually did bring danger into this house that had already seen too much bloodshed.

No. She was being foolish. The phantom had been a figment of her overwrought imagination. Helene Ledger was as dead as the flowers in her forsaken garden.

But if the ghost was real, then so were her warnings. Death was bearing down on Collette.

She forced herself to stay in bed until the sun

peeked over the horizon and dropped golden rays of light into the garden outside her window.

Sliding her bare feet into her slippers, Collette opened the door and stepped into the hall. The house was silent except for the ticking of the large clock in the family room and a vibrating snore coming from one of the bedrooms.

She stopped in the kitchen for a glass of water and tried to shake the sense of imminent doom. When that didn't help, she opted for the serenity she'd found on the front porch before her brother had shown up with all his bluster and threats.

She closed the door behind her and shivered at the howls of a pack of coyotes in the distance and a rustle in the grass just beyond the porch. She followed the sound with her gaze and spotted a family of skunks parading by, no doubt returning from a night of scavenging. She stayed perfectly still until they'd disappeared from view and the chance of inciting an odorous attack had passed.

A black spider crept by her foot. She stepped over it and walked to the edge of the porch. The wind had picked up, and the limbs in a nearby tree creaked like an old man's bones.

All of a sudden, she had the crazy feeling that she was being watched. She'd best get a grip before she saw ghosts coming at her from all directions.

Shoving her hands in her pockets, she took one last look into the scrubby brush where the skunks had disappeared. Another rustle, much louder that the first, came from somewhere near the woodshed. She stared in that direction and spotted a glint of sunlight bouncing off metal.

Collette turned to go back inside just as the crack of gunfire shattered the early morning quiet.

Chapter Eleven

Dylan woke instantly at the sound of gunfire, jumping from the bed as adrenaline rushed through his veins and triggered his battle instincts. Only this time he wasn't in a combat zone. His senses became razor sharp, his mind sizing up the situation as he grabbed the pistol he'd left on his bedside table and tore down the hall in his underwear. The scream had come from outside, though he had no idea why Collette would be outside this early in the morning.

By the time he reached the front door, Collette was inside and leaning against it. Her robe was open enough that he could tell she had nothing on beneath it. His senses reeled, but his gaze was drawn to the blood trickling down her cheek and the ghostly pallor of her face.

He stroked the injured cheek with his free hand. Her skin was icy cold, but the injury was no more than a scratch, likely made by one of the splintered wood fragments that clung to her robe. "Are you hurt?"

"I don't think so," she said, her voice quivering. "But someone just tried to kill me."

"Did you see the shooter?"

"No, but a split second before the shot, I saw a glint of sun off metal out by the woodshed. I think what I saw was a gun."

She yanked her robe tightly around her just as Troy joined them, still zipping his jeans.

"Was that gunfire?"

"Someone's on the property," Dylan said. "Take care of Collette. I'm going after him."

"No, Dylan, please," Collette pleaded. "Call 911. He has a gun."

That made two of them. "Stay inside," he ordered and rushed out the door. Fury drove him, but his brain and training kicked into autopilot. He jumped from the porch and raced to the tree line that stretched almost to the old woodshed.

There was more gunfire, and one of the bullets ricocheted off the trunk of a pine tree just in front of him. Dylan ran even faster, staying in the cover of trees, his bare feet almost silent in the thick grass.

His breathing came hard as he neared the woodshed. The last few yards he'd be in the open. He needed to draw the shooter out so he could get a clear shot to take him down, hopefully without killing him. Dead men didn't talk and he wanted answers.

An engine sputtered, knocked and backfired. Damn. The shooter was back in his vehicle, giving up and making a run for it. Dylan dashed toward the shed, but before he reached it, he spotted a man on a motorbike heading for the east pasture. Unless Dylan came up with a better plan, the son of a bitch was going to get away.

He sprinted back toward the house, stepping in a patch of stickers that punctured his skin. The sharp pains only urged him faster.

Troy was on the porch, holding the rifle he must have retrieved from Dylan's truck. "He escaped on a motorbike," Dylan yelled. "I'm going after him."

"Take this with you." Troy started toward the truck with the rifle.

"You keep it in case he doubles back here," Dylan called.

"I don't need it," Troy said. "I have a shotgun inside the house." He opened the passenger-side door of Dylan's truck and left the rifle with Dylan.

Dylan didn't know if Troy's having a firearm was legal under the circumstances of his release, but he didn't have time to worry about that now.

Collette came running out of the house still in her robe.

"Get back inside," Dylan ordered.

She kept coming, jumping into the truck and grabbing the rifle as he fired the ignition. She slammed the door. "What are you waiting on? Hit the gas before the dirty rotten coward gets away."

"Buckle up," he said, knowing there was no time and probably no use to argue with her. "And for God's sake, don't shoot yourself or me with that rifle."

COLLETTE'S FRIGHT was swiftly replaced by the need to keep the rifle and her body from bouncing off the roof as Dylan's truck rumbled and rocked across the bumpy hills. The would-be killer had a head start, but he couldn't be too far ahead of them.

"That way," Collette yelled, pointing to the left when she noticed a downed fence.

"Good work."

Dylan drove through the break, dragging down more fence posts before cutting across empty pastureland at breakneck speed. The bent and broken grass blades made the shooter's trail easy to follow, but there was still no sign of the motorbike.

In spite of the danger and the gravity of the

situation, exhilaration rushed Collette's system like a drug.

"I never realized riding shotgun through empty pastures would be this exciting."

"Don't get used to it," Dylan said. "It's hell on the tires."

They came to another downed fence, but this one opened to the blacktop road that ran behind the ranch. Tracks from the motorbike's tires led right up to the road and then swerved right.

Dylan turned left.

"You turned the wrong way," she squealed.

"My guess is he knew I'd follow and he was trying to point me in the opposite direction."

"Okay, makes sense," she admitted and wondered why she was so naive when it came to the criminal mind.

"Besides, going left would get him to the highway a lot quicker," Dylan added.

They drove another ten miles without any sign of the bike. When they reached the highway, Dylan slowed to a stop, muttering a few choice curses under his breath.

"Sorry for the soldier talk," he said. "It's just aggravating to lose the guy when we all but had him in our sights."

"Are you giving up?"

"For the moment. The guy could have gone in any direction or cut off across someone else's land. We could keep going but we'd just be chasing rabbits."

"Instead of the rat we need." She felt the frustration herself, but sitting here in the truck at daybreak, holding a rifle steady with one hand and trying to keep her robe together with the other, she couldn't help but see the humor in this. Her smile drew an instant reaction.

"You could have been killed back there, Collette. Exactly what is it you find amusing about this?"

"Us. You in your underwear. Me riding shotgun half-naked. You have to admit we make an unusual crime-fighter team. Maybe we should try for a TV reality show."

He snaked an arm around her shoulders. "You, Collette McGuire, have gone mad from your wild and daring ride."

"No, Dylan." She reached over and circled his navel with her index finger. "I'm giddy from the excitement of you."

He leaned in close, his lips brushing her eyelids, her nose, her cheeks, as her thrill quotient went soaring to a new high. When his lips finally took hers, she was almost to the point of begging.

He ravaged her mouth, the kisses frantic at first and punctuated by tantalizing thrusts of his tongue. Finally the kisses grew deeper, and she melted into them, savoring the salty sweetness and the passion.

Her robe opened. Dylan slipped his hand inside and she tensed at the delicious thrill of the touch of his fingers on her bare skin. She arched toward him as he cupped her breasts and let his thumbs massage her taut nipples.

Soft moans of pleasure emanated from deep in her throat. Heat rushed to her core and she entangled one hand in the hair at his temples and splayed the other across his abdomen.

"Who knew?" she whispered.

"Knew what?"

"That having a private protector could feel this good."

"It's not supposed to. Definitely not supposed to." He pulled away and ran both hands through his hair as if he were annoyed, or just plain frustrated.

"We better get back." His words were husky, his breath ragged.

"Did I say something to upset you?"

"No, but I need my mind clear to keep you safe and my mind is never going to be clear when I'm this turned on by you."

Dylan had put her on a sensual high the moment he'd shown up back in Mustang Run, but he was right. They should back away from each other, but not for the reason he thought. Nightmare or reality, Helene had warned Collette that she was pulling her family into danger. Nothing proved that more than the fact that Dylan had gone after a madman.

Collette had not only dragged Dylan into her perilous mire but she was entangling him in complications that couldn't be good for him or Troy. No matter how crazy she was about Dylan, the best thing she could do for him and Troy was to get out of their lives until her stalker was behind bars.

TROY TOYED WITH the 30-06 bullet he'd dug from the support post with his new pocket knife. The knife was another staple Able had provided, same as he'd supplied the shotgun. Guns, knives, ropes, machetes, all just tools of the trade to a rancher, but foreign and illicit to a prisoner.

When Able had first handed him the gun, Troy had broken out in a cold sweat. Even handling the knife seemed strange after all these years, and it had taken him several minutes to angle the blade and work the bullet from the wood.

The bullet had burrowed in just about head high. Had it struck Collette, her brain would have splintered and sprayed the porch the way the slivers of old wood had. The shooter had been aiming to kill.

Memories flooded Troy's mind, trapping him

in the horror and the nauseating visions he'd never even tried to escape. To let his pain and wrath dim would negate the gravity of the crime and devalue Helene's life. He would never let that happen, and he would never let his heartbreak heal until whoever had killed her paid for the crime.

Helene had been home alone when her killer had come calling, and the hooligan hadn't shot her from a distance. He'd walked inside the house and shot her twice in the head and once in the chest at point-blank range. Three shots when any one of them would have killed her.

Excessive brutality indicated a crime of passion, the prosecutor had said when he'd argued the case against Troy. His wife had been leaving him and taking their sons with her. Faced with the loss of all that he loved, Troy had given in to his darker side.

The side of him his mother-in-law had claimed Helene knew all too well. That's why Helene had warned her parents that under no circumstances were they to confront Troy about anything to do with the ranch or money.

The accusations hadn't fazed Troy then. Nothing had. The pain had deadened him to everything except the knowledge that he'd never see Helene again, never hold her slender, beautiful body in his arms. Never hear her sing when she was working around the house or in her garden, never dance with her under the light of the moon or two-step her around the kitchen.

Never be able to whisper how much he loved her and have her whisper the words back to him.

Some lunatic had robbed him of that.

Now another lunatic was after Collette. But why? The stalker story didn't hack it. Not when two days ago the anonymous caller was professing his love for Collette, and now he was shooting at her.

He could be someone who didn't stand out but faded easily into a crowd. A man whom Collette might have seen many times in passing and never really noticed. Even in prison there had been guys like that, the ones who didn't attract the attention of the guards or the bullies.

Those were the lucky ones.

If this guy was that nondescript, it could take weeks or months to expose him.

In the meantime, Dylan was putting his life on the line, and not just from the sniper who'd tried to take him and Collette out this morning. If Collette had taken that bullet, Glenn McGuire would have battered Dylan with questions until he was too weary to think, would have focused on every idle word he uttered and every dubious act he'd ever committed.

All that for no reason except that Dylan was the son of Troy Ledger.

But Troy would not let Dylan become another sacrificial lamb to Glenn McGuire's need for revenge. He'd make damned sure of that. For now he just wished Dylan and Collette would get back here so he'd know they were safe.

Too restless and anxious to sit back and do nothing, Troy headed toward the woodshed.

He scanned the area as he covered the distance. A large black rat scurried over the top of a pile of rotting firewood stacked outside the dilapidated shed. A loose strip of tattered metal hung just above the wood, the remains of an old sign advertising a cleaning product that hadn't been manufactured in years.

Just below the sign, Troy spotted a smear of color.

Fresh blood from a scratch the stalker had gotten from the prickly brush that had overgrown the shed? Or from the rusted metal of the sign?

Possibly.

His spirits lifted. He just might have discovered the shooter's DNA.

Other than having Dylan at home, it was the most positive thing that had happened since he'd returned to Mustang Run. Even Glenn McGuire with all his ploys and vindictiveness couldn't ignore DNA.

SIX DEPUTIES CAME barreling down the ranch road shortly after Collette and Dylan returned from the chase. Her father was not with the group, and she suspected it was because he hadn't been informed of the situation. Fortunately, both she and Dylan had had time to slip into more appropriate attire before the lawmen arrived.

Troy had called in and reported the shooting and the fact that he had found what was likely the culprit's blood near his woodshed. If it turned out the DNA was in the FBI's CODIS base, they'd have the identity of the shooter. It was the most promising development since the attack.

At a quarter past nine the second piece of welcoming news arrived via cell phone. Eleanor was alert, cognizant and asking to see Collette.

By eleven, she and Dylan were standing just outside the door to Eleanor's private room. The young police officer on guard introduced himself as Clay Sevier and flashed his badge.

"I'll need to check your IDs before you can enter Room 612."

They each gave Clay their driver's licenses. He studied them carefully. "Are you related to Sheriff McGuire?" he asked as he handed the license back to Collette.

"He's my father."

"A good man. I met him yesterday when he came by to talk to the patient."

She nodded, avoiding comment.

The guard frowned as he returned Dylan's driver's license. "Collette is cleared to visit Ms. Baker, but I'll have to ask you to wait outside."

"That's better anyway," Collette assured Dylan. "Eleanor will feel more comfortable and free to talk if I'm by myself." She turned back to the officer. "Is anyone in the room with her now?"

"Not at the moment. Her mother was in there most of the morning, but she left about ten minutes ago. I believe she was going to get something to eat."

"I could use a cup of coffee and a newspaper," Dylan said. He put a hand on Collette's shoulder. "I'll make a quick run to the cafeteria and then come back and wait on you here."

"Take your time, but cross your fingers that we leave the hospital with a description of Eleanor's attacker."

"They're crossed, but don't count on too much. The doctor said it could take days—or even longer—for her to remember everything."

"I know."

"Call if you need me," Dylan said.

"I will." She tapped lightly on the door to Eleanor's room. When there was no answer, she pushed it open and walked inside.

Collette's heart sank to her toes when she saw how wiped out Eleanor looked in the oversize hospital gown. Her eyes were closed, but rimmed in dark circles. An IV fed into one arm. The opposite shoulder was bandaged.

Eleanor's hair had been combed and pushed behind her ears, but it looked flat and dull, lacking its usual shine and vibrancy. The same could be said of Eleanor. Except that Eleanor hadn't *lost* hers. It had been stolen from her by the thug she prayed Eleanor was about to describe.

Eleanor groaned and slapped at the cover without waking. Collette stepped to the side of the bed, not sure if she should disturb her. A nurse walked in the room, saw Collette and smiled.

"Look, Eleanor. You have company."

Eleanor opened her eyes as the nurse checked her pulse. Her gaze settled on Collette and she managed a weak smile.

Collette fit her hand on top of Eleanor's. "Hi, girl. You're looking good. Nice gown."

"You think? I can probably filch you one."

"I'd take you up on that if it were my color."

The nurse finished her check. "You two have a good visit, but don't tire out my patient," she cautioned as she left them alone.

"Guess I made a mess of your house," Eleanor said. "Teach you to befriend an investigative reporter."

Her words came slow and slightly labored, but her wit was intact. Collette was certain that was a good sign.

"I'm so sorry you were attacked," Collette said. "If I'd had any idea you were in danger at my place, I would have never invited you to stay over."

"Not your fault. Just luck of the draw."

Collette seriously doubted that. "Do you feel like talking about the attack?"

"I feel okay. They have good drugs in this place."

"I'll bet."

Eleanor shifted and winced. Obviously the meds didn't relieve all the pain.

"I was in the living room, drinking wine and watching CSI reruns. Had the volume too loud, I guess. Didn't hear him break in."

"Did he come into the living room?"

She shook her head, a slight movement, but enough. "I'd made myself a BLT. I took my empty plate back to the kitchen and there he was."

Lurking in Collette's kitchen the way he'd been lurking in her life. Collette felt that sinking, violated feeling again. Eleanor had to feel that, too, along with her pain. "Did he say anything before he attacked you?"

"I'm not sure. The attack is still fuzzy. I

remember screaming and him diving at me with a kitchen knife." Eleanor squinted and then closed her eyes for a few seconds before opening them again and looking right at Collette. "I'm lucky to be alive."

"Yes, you are. Thank God for that." But the monster might not have given up on killing her yet. He could be in the hospital this very minute, walking the halls, waiting for any opportunity to kill Eleanor before she talked. He had to be stopped.

"Did you get a good look at the man?"

"I must have, but all I can remember is that he was tall. And burly. You know, muscled."

"Was he wearing a ski mask or gloves?"

"Gloves. He was wearing gloves. Black ones. I'd forgotten about that."

So Eleanor's memory did respond to coaxing. Collette would have to keep wheedling unless Eleanor grew stressed by her attempts.

"Was he wearing anything over his face?"

"Maybe. I can't remember. I had to have seen him, but I just can't remember."

"What about his hair? Was it long or short?"

Eleanor sucked in her bottom lip and touched a finger to her chin. "I don't know. I just don't know."

"Any idea if he was young, old, middle-aged?"

Finally she smiled again. "Not old enough. I could have beaten up an elderly man."

"I'd have paid to see that," Collette teased, though she wasn't ready to let up on the pressure completely just yet. "Was he older than I am?"

"Could have been older. But he was strong. Really strong."

"Do you remember anything else about him? Scars, tattoos, a beard?"

"It happened fast. Wham, bam."

"What did he say to you?"

"Nothing. I don't think he said anything. He stabbed me. I was on the floor—for a long time, I think. Then we heard you drive up."

"Is that when he hit you over the head?"

"No. He had a gun. When you drove up, he had a gun."

"There was a vehicle," Collette explained, "but it wasn't mine. Dylan Ledger drove up in his truck. He got there before I did. He's the one who found you unconscious on the kitchen floor."

"Dylan Ledger, the murderer's son?"

"Dylan Ledger, my friend," Collette corrected.

"Why was he there?"

"I invited him."

"Huh?"

"I invited him to stop by anytime," Collette repeated. "He took me up on the invitation."

Eleanor shook her head. "Don't trust him."

"I do trust him." She was even starting to trust Helene. Eleanor and Melinda were probably the only two people she knew who would believe her tale about conversing with a paranormal spirit, but she didn't want to say anything now that might further confuse Eleanor.

"What happened after he pulled the gun?" Collette asked.

"He was going to kill you. I had to stop him."

"How?"

"With the skillet. It was still on the range. I pulled myself up and grabbed it."

"Did you hit him with it?"

"I'm not sure. The skillet was in my hand. That's the last thing I remember."

"He may have taken it away from you and hit you instead. That would explain the concussion and the knot on your head."

"He was strong."

"Are you sure he didn't say anything? Do you remember a gravelly, gruff voice?" She was leading the witness, but it wasn't as if she was in a courtroom. She was trying to find a villainous pervert.

"I don't remember. I'm sorry, Collette." Eleanor closed her eyes and turned away.

Collette had pushed as hard as she dared.

"Don't try to think about the attack for now, Eleanor. Just rest and take care of yourself."

Eleanor didn't respond. The meds were doing their work, and she was drifting off to sleep. "It will all work out," Collette whispered before she made her way to the door. But if it didn't work out soon, the guy was going to strike again.

He'd gone along for months with nothing but phone calls, but now it seemed he'd become desperate. There had to be an explanation for that.

Her father was steps from Eleanor's door when Collette exited, in a quiet but animated discussion with the cop on guard duty. She was tempted to march right by him without speaking, but the situation they were in was too serious to let the long-held resentments interfere.

"There's your daughter," Clay said.

Her father turned to face her. "So it is, though she hasn't acted much like a daughter of late."

"I just talked to Eleanor," she said, refusing to fight with him here. "She's conscious, but still under the effects of the medication."

"Did she give you a description of the perp?"

"Only that he was tall and muscled. She just drifted off to sleep, but I can tell you everything she said."

"Then the information would only be hearsay."

Dylan walked up and joined them, newspaper tucked under his arm and coffee in hand. Her father glared at him, clenching his fists as if preparing to throw a punch. Subtlety wasn't in his repertoire.

She was sure Dylan noticed, but he gave no indication that he cared.

"Good morning, Sheriff."

Her father ignored his greeting and pointed a condemning finger at Collette. "I see you're still playing your silly little games and putting yourself in danger. You just can't listen, can you, Mildred?"

Mildred. Collette swallowed hard as the mistake sent a new round of resentment swirling inside her. He'd not only called her by her mother's name but used the same tone he'd used with her mother so many times before.

She turned and strode away before she said what she was thinking and caused a scene. Dylan caught up with her just as she stepped into the crowded elevator.

"What was that about?"

"Too much to go into now."

The elevator stopped on the fourth floor, and two men and a woman stepped on. The doors were already closing behind them when Collette heard a hoarse, croaky voice coming from outside the elevator. Her blood ran cold. She'd know that voice anywhere.

Chapter Twelve

Collette tried to reach through a cluster of people to hit the Door Open button, but it was too late. The doors had closed tight, and the elevator had already begun its descent. When the elevator stopped at the third floor, she grabbed Dylan's arm and tugged him off even while a lady with two young children was pushing into the car.

Dylan's brows arched. "Change of plans?"

"The gruff voice. That was him. My stalker."

"You heard his voice?"

"Yes, just as those people were getting on at the fourth floor." She looked around for stairs.

Dylan spotted the stairwell sign first, took her hand and took off running.

Once in the stairwell, he let her take the lead, only jumping in front of her when they reached the door to the fourth floor. He pushed it open and waited for her to exit.

"The elevators are right there," Dylan said, pointing to his right.

The hallway was empty. Disappointment settled like a bowling ball in her stomach. "If he was waiting for an elevator, he may have already boarded one and disappeared."

"But we don't know that he was getting on an elevator, only that he was close enough that you heard his voice. Do you have any feel for the direction the voice came from?"

"I thought it came from the left, but I can't be sure."

"Tell me how Eleanor described him."

"Tall, muscled, strong. That's it."

With little to go on, they hurried down the halls but saw no one who looked or sounded suspicious. Collette's confidence in finding the man was sinking fast.

"Let's try the sixth floor," Dylan urged.

"But I heard him on this floor."

"Saying what?"

"'Excuse me.' He said, 'Excuse me,' and then he coughed."

"He could have been on another elevator, one stopped on the fourth floor on its climb to the sixth."

Of course. She should have thought of that. And right at that very moment he could be on his way to Room 612. "Let's go."

They took the stairs, and Collette was panting by the time they'd run the two flights. Again, the hall near the stairwell was empty, and no one was waiting at the elevators. They hurried toward Eleanor's room, where the guard was chatting up a pert, young nurse with ample curves.

Collette breathed a little easier. If there had been trouble, surely he wouldn't be carrying on a flirtation.

"Go wait with the guard while I check out the men's room," Dylan told her. "If I see someone who looks suspicious, I'll ask him a question and see if he croaks like a bullfrog."

"It's not quite that bad," she admitted. "But if he sounds like he has a cold, nab him."

The nurse walked away from Clay Sevier, and Collette quickly caught up and fell in step with her. "My friend was supposed to meet me here ten minutes ago—a tall guy, gruff voice."

"I haven't seen him. Who are you here to visit?"

"Eleanor Baker."

"If I see a guy who looks lost, I'll send him that way."

"Thanks." Collette's frustration built.

Dylan met up with her before she reached Eleanor's room. "No luck," he said, "but I do have an idea."

"Good. I'm desperate for one."

"Assuming your father is still with Eleanor, you need to let him know what's going on. He can initiate a room search to see if anyone's on the floor without a legitimate reason."

"Why didn't I think of that?"

"If you thought of everything on your own, you wouldn't need me."

She was certain that she would.

The guard smiled as they approached him. "Back so soon?"

"Yes, I need to discuss something with my father."

"He's with the patient, and he said I was to keep visitors out until he was finished questioning her."

"What I have to tell him concerns the attack and it can't wait."

"Orders are orders," the guard said.

"This is an emergency. I'll take full responsibility for the consequences." She hurried past him and eased open the door to Eleanor's room.

"But you admit you were warned to stop digging into the murder. Who else but one of the Ledgers would be alarmed by what you planned to write?"

"Someone with something to hide," Eleanor murmured.

"Or someone trying to protect the guilty," the sheriff said. "A son, maybe."

"Like Dylan?"

"Exactly."

Collette started to shake. How dare he try to frame Dylan for the attack when he knew her stalker had called from this very hospital just yesterday.

The guard propped a hand over the door frame. "Step away from the door."

"I have to see you, Dad," she called out, ignoring Clay.

The sheriff left Eleanor's bedside. "What's the problem here?"

"I have to talk to you about the case. It's urgent." Her voice vibrated with rage that he'd been going after Dylan. She struggled to get it under control until the current emergency was handled.

The sheriff nodded to the guard. "It's okay. She can come in."

"We can't talk in there," Collette protested. "We need privacy."

"What's this about?"

"Please, just step outside with me."

He followed her into the hallway. When he saw Dylan, he stiffened, but this time he gave the sarcasm a rest.

She led him a few feet away so that they had a small degree of privacy. "I'm almost certain my stalker is in the hospital now and probably hiding somewhere on this floor."

"Do you have evidence to that fact, or is this some tomfool idea you got from Dylan?"

"I heard his voice. I think he was on a different elevator, going up when we were going down."

"A lot of voices sound the same, especially at a distance."

"It was him, Dad. As many times as I've been tormented by that voice, I'd know it anywhere."

"Okay, take it easy. I'll look into this. You do realize I'm out of my jurisdiction."

"It's not out of Clay Sevier's. He or his supervisor could have the staff check all the patient rooms and supply closets or any other place the goon might be hiding."

"Are you telling me how to do my job now?"

"No, of course not." She knew better than to try and tell him anything. Beg or inveigle, he loved that. But never tell.

"I'll handle this, Collette. Feel free to leave and take Dylan Ledger with you."

"I need to be here," she insisted. "I'm the only one who can identify the voice."

"Then have Dylan take you to the coffee shop. If something comes of the search, I'll call you."

More proof that he didn't actually consider Dylan a suspect or a danger to her. Yet he was determined to make Dylan's stay in Mustang Run so exasperating that he gave up and left. Or maybe it was Troy Ledger he wanted to run out of town.

"Fine," she said. "Find the stalker and you'll have Eleanor's attacker."

"If he's here, I'll find him. As for his arrest solving the assault case, that's yet to be determined. Bear in mind that the stalker called for months without resorting to violence. The attack came the very day the Ledgers moved back to town."

COLLETTE AND DYLAN chose the hospital's multilevel atrium instead of the coffee shop. Live plants and sunshine were far more conducive than caffeine to releasing the stress and lowering the levels of adrenaline rushing through her veins.

They strolled for a minute and then Collette dropped to an ornate wooden bench that faced a sparkling fountain. Dylan sat next to her, resting his arm along the arched back.

"It's beautiful here," she admitted, "but I'd rather be on the sixth floor in the middle of the action."

"That makes two of us, but even if we were there, we wouldn't be allowed access to any area but the restrooms and the halls."

She leaned back and Dylan let his hand fall to her shoulder and his thumb trail the tight tendons in her neck. It was amazing how in sync she felt with him when he'd only dropped into her life two days ago. Great for her. Not so terrific for him.

"You must wish you'd waited until next week to arrive in town," she said. "Then you would have missed the chaos."

"Nope. I'm glad I arrived exactly when I did."

"Me, too. After talking to Eleanor, I've even more convinced that you saved both our lives by showing up at my house when you did."

"I can't take a lot of credit for that. I was just coming by to intrude on your evening."

"Timing is everything." She'd promised herself last night that she'd gracefully bow out of his life before she dragged him into more danger. That was probably even more critical today with her father determined to make things hard on him.

Helene Ledger's ghost would no doubt be happy about Collette leaving Dylan's life. She suspected that Troy Ledger would as well, though he'd made her feel welcome and even cooked her breakfast this morning while she'd dressed for her run to the hospital.

"I still fear that spending so much time with me gives you very little time to bond with your father," Collette said.

"I'm not sure how much bonding we'd be doing

anyway. He spends most of the time staring out the back window or standing at the door of the bedroom he shared with my mother."

"He's been away from the ranch and cut off from society for nearly eighteen years. The re-adjustment must be difficult for him."

"I'm sure it is. Readjusting to civilian life after eight years in the service was difficult enough. Actually dealing with the stalker situation has crystallized a couple of decisions about what I'd like to do next in my life."

If one of the decisions was to run as far as he could from Mustang Run, she didn't want to hear it. Still, she had to ask. "What decisions have you made?"

"I definitely don't want to go into any type of law enforcement."

"Had you been considering that as a career option?"

"I'd talked about the possibility with Wyatt. He loves it and thought I should give it a try."

"All law-enforcement officers are not as intolerable as my father if that's what's holding you back."

"No. I've just had enough violence and bureaucracy—all of the things that would go with the job. I gave a hundred percent during my eight years in the service. I'm glad I was able to do that for my country, but I'm ready to move on."

She experienced a plummeting sensation that didn't mix well with the chaos of the morning and the interminable wait to hear news from her father.

"To move on as in away from Mustang Run?"

"Not necessarily. I'm thinking of going into ranching, either here with Dad or on a spread of my own. I have a small inheritance from my maternal grandfather and I saved most of my salary while I was in Iraq."

"You made that decision after only two days?"

"It doesn't take long to know when something's right."

His tone made her think he could be talking about more than just ranching. Warmth seeped into every pore. It could just be infatuation, but her feelings for Dylan were growing stronger by the second.

Dylan shifted and moved away from her. She wondered if he, too, was feeling the heat.

"Guess I've always been a cowboy at heart," he said.

"I could have told you that from the moment I met you."

"Really, Miss Personality Expert. How's that?"

"You had that cowboy swagger when you

walked up on the steps of the ranch house and tipped your hat to the waiting sharks. Besides, you know the old adage, don't call him a cowboy until you see him ride. I saw you ride, and you're a natural with horses."

"How am I doing with you?"

"You've got potential," she teased.

Dylan pushed up his shirt sleeve and looked at his watch. It finally hit her that the conversation over the past few minutes had been designed to keep her mind off the drama playing out on the sixth floor.

It had worked for a few minutes, but the anxiety had just come crashing down on her again.

She stretched her legs in front of her, crossing her ankles and flexing her toes to release the coiled strain to her muscles.

"I really appreciate all you've done for me, Dylan, but the best thing I can do for you and your father right now is to get out of your lives."

"I thought we were past that."

"I thought so, too, but things with my father will just continuously get worse for you until this case is solved."

Dylan turned to her and cupped her face in his hands, forcing her to look in his eyes.

"Get this straight in your head right now, Collette. I've faced enemies whose idea of destruction was blowing me into a thousand pieces or cutting off my head and hanging it from a pole. I'm not afraid of your father. Your walking out of my life is the last thing I need or want. If it's what you want, I'll live with it, but don't even think it would be best for me."

He dropped his hands from her face, then took one of her hands in his. "What is it with you and your father? Every meeting between the two of you is charged with hostility. You can't even talk about him without getting edgy and tense."

"We've had our differences."

"It must have been a hell of a difference to leave you this bitter."

"You don't want to go there, Dylan."

"You don't have to tell me anything you don't want to, but it would help me get a grip on what's going on."

She took in a deep breath and exhaled slowly. "Okay, Dylan, I'll dish the dirt, but I have to warn you. My family history is sordid and heartrending."

Dylan squeezed her hand. "Welcome to my world."

Chapter Thirteen

"The accident that led to my mother's stroke could have been avoided."

Dylan kept hold of Collette's hand, knowing the worst was yet to come. Yet if she didn't get the rage and resentment out in the open, he feared she might explode, especially with the incidents of the past two days no doubt setting her nerves on a short fuse.

"Mom asked me to come home for spring break my senior year, saying there was something important she needed to tell me," Collette continued. "I knew from her voice that something was seriously wrong, but she refused to say more on the phone. I immediately thought cancer or some type of risky operation, and I canceled my Florida plans. I was a wreck the rest of the week."

"Had she been diagnosed with a life-threatening condition?"

"No. Our visit turned into a true-confessions

session for which I was totally unprepared. I knew living with Dad's belligerence wasn't easy. He and I had clashed on many occasions, but he never seemed to get to Mom the way he did me. That's why I was totally unprepared for the bomb she dropped on me."

"The divorce bomb?"

"How did you guess?"

"I witnessed it more than once in the service with guys who had never seen it coming. One day they're telling you about the wonderful wife and kids back home, the next they're reading Dear John."

"Mom said that she'd had all she could take of my father and that she'd only stayed with him the last few years because of me. She wanted me to graduate and be on my own before she left him."

Which basically made Collette the scapegoat for her mother's bad marriage. Talk about piling on the guilt. And Dylan could imagine all holy hell breaking out when Glenn McGuire found out he was being dumped.

"How did the sheriff react to the prospect of divorce?" he asked her.

"Mom hadn't told him and didn't plan to until she was ready to walk out the door. She said she knew he would explode and that there would be no living in the same house with him after that."

"So you were the first to know?"

"I think so, but that wasn't the half of it. She said my brother was conceived out of wedlock and that even after Dad had said he loved her and asked her to marry him, he'd still been writing to an old girlfriend begging her to take him back."

"How did she discover that?"

"Apparently the woman returned all the letters to Dad with a note asking him to stop writing. Mother found them in the attic when she was going through some of Dad's college yearbooks. The letters were important enough to him that he kept them all those years, and believe me, Dad is not the sentimental sort."

"What did he say when she confronted him?"

"She didn't. That's my Mom. She hated conflict and avoided it at all costs, but I think the letters were the real impetus for deciding to leave him. She insisted I read the letters."

"And did you?"

Collette shook her head. "They were Dad's property. I wouldn't have felt right. I refused to take them, but she stashed them in my luggage without my knowing it before I went back to UT."

"What did you do with them?"

"I still have them. I've thought of returning them to Dad, but that would mean having a conversation with him about them, and I've never wanted to deal with that."

"How do the accident and strokes fit in with her wanting a divorce?"

Collette's shoulders sagged, and she dropped her head to stare at the toe of her right boot that she was twisting as if putting out a lit cigarette.

"I only know the rest from what Dad told me. I heard about the accident just as I'd finished my last final. Dad had gone in to work early that day to deal with a case of vandalism at the high-school football stadium. He'd gotten caught in a sudden spring thunderstorm and had gone home to change into dry clothes. When he got there, Mom was packing her bags."

Rotten way to find out your wife was leaving, Dylan thought. He wouldn't even wish that on a hardheaded, cantankerous guy like the sheriff. Not that he was taking sides.

"Dad confronted her and they had an argument. His story is that he tried to grab her arm to keep her from leaving before they had a chance to talk things out. She slung a duffel at him and slipped in the process, falling down the steps and banging the back of her head against the heavy antique bell stand in the corner of the landing. When they got to the hospital the doctors told him she had a concussion. From there it went from bad to tragic."

"Was your mother conscious?"

"No, and when she was still unconscious the next day, they did a CAT scan that showed brain contusions. I rushed home from Austin, though they were still telling us she'd be okay."

Collette's voice grew shaky. Her hands had grown clammy, and she pulled them from his and wiped them on her jeans.

"We can finish this conversation later," Dylan said. "I should have never asked when you have so much else to deal with."

"I'd like to finish it now," she said, her gaze straight ahead. She pulled her arms tight around her chest. "I've never talked about this with anyone else, not even Bill. I think maybe it's time."

"Then I'm glad I'm here."

"Thanks." She propped her elbow on the arm of the bench and supported her head with her hand. "Mom remained in the ICU and they kept her sedated so that her brain could rest. When she came to, she recognized me and Dad and talked to both of us, though she avoided mentioning her fall or the divorce. But then, so did we. It didn't seem the right time for it.

"I left the hospital that night, thinking all was well, but then she slipped into a coma during the night. An MRI the next morning indicated vasospasms."

"I'm not familiar with that."

"Constriction of the blood vessels that limit blood to the brain. As a result of that there were clear signs that she'd suffered multiple strokes."

Dylan had known several guys who'd had brain contusions, both on his high-school hockey team and in the service. None had ever had strokes or any lasting complications. "Are strokes normal after brain contusions?"

"No, the neurologist said he'd seen it occur after aneurysms, but it's extremely rare after contusions. But it does happen. It *did* happen. Mom never recovered. She died a few days later."

Collette's head fell against his shoulder, and she cratered against him as the emotional strain drained her body of strength. The friction between her and her father made sense to him now. She blamed him for the accident and her mother's resulting death. She had never let herself forgive him.

Dylan was far from an expert on family dissension, but he'd lived with it for years. That's how he knew that family ties could hold against most anything the world threw at them. Those ties were why he was back in Mustang Run. They were why he was trying to find some way to connect with his father.

They were why Collette needed to let go of the blame and hostility and go on with her life. Unless she believed the fall wasn't an accident.

"I know Dad didn't intentionally push Mom down the stairs," Collette said, as if reading his mind. "But—"

Her cell phone rang, yanking them both back to the problem at hand. "It's Dad," she said, sitting up straight and pushing her back against the wooden slats of the bench. She answered the call with a question. "Have you found Eleanor's attacker?"

Dylan didn't have to hear the answers to get the gist of them. Disappointment and frustration were written all over Collette's face. Sitting around, doing nothing while they waited for the next attack was never good battle strategy.

Fortunately, Dylan had a plan.

It was just after two-thirty when Collette and Dylan pulled up in front of her house. They'd stopped for lunch at a roadside restaurant on the way back from the hospital. As usual, she'd nibbled at her meal, leaving more than half of the Texas-size bacon/jalapeño burger on the plate.

Dylan had devoured all of his along with a side of onion rings, and washed it all down with a tall glass of iced tea. She liked watching him eat. He did it with such relish.

In fact she liked everything about him. It was

completely out of character for her to fall this hard, this fast. But then she'd never met a man like Dylan Ledger.

Tough as nails, yet thoughtful. Protective, but not domineering. And so incredibly sexy and virile that he took her breath away even in a crisis.

"We can just pick up your appointment book and take it back to the ranch if you'd rather clear out of here," Dylan said.

She pushed her key into her front-door lock. "I usually keep it with me, but in all the confusion, I forgot it when I changed handbags yesterday. I'm fine to work here. I don't see Sukey's car, so she must be done with the cleaning."

Collette opened the door, and they were greeted by a house that was so clean it sparkled and was fragrant with the fresh scent of flowers. She didn't have to look far to find them. A huge bouquet of spring blossoms in brilliant pink, snowy white and vivid red sat in the middle of the antique chest that served as coffee table. She recognized the vase as one of her own.

"Alma must have sent the flowers with Sukey," Collette said, walking over for a better look at the bouquet. "It's not something Bill would think to do."

Dylan grabbed her arm as she reached for the card.

"Let me get that for you."

"I'm not help—" She broke off the sentence as she saw him carefully touch only the edges of the card. He thought they could be from the stalker. But the man had never sent flowers or gifts before.

Dylan murmured a couple of choice sentiments under his breath. That told her all she needed to know.

"They're from *him,* aren't they?"

"Yeah. He's either a complete psycho or there's method to his madness."

"Which would you guess?"

"The latter," Dylan admitted.

He held the card so that Collette could read it without touching it, just in case there were fingerprints. She doubted there were. The man had outfoxed them at every turn. No reason to think he'd screw up now.

So sorry about your friend. I can't sleep for thinking it could have been you. I couldn't bear to see you in pain. Take care, my sweet Collette. We'll talk soon.

Her blood boiled. "I can't believe his gall to just walk in and out of my house like this."

"Wait here," Dylan said.

Her pulse quickened as he rushed past her and

to the back of the house. Did Dylan think the stalker was still here? What if he was?

What if he'd come straight here from the hospital and arrived while Sukey was cleaning? What if Dylan found her lying on the floor in a pool of blood?

Collette rushed toward the kitchen. Dylan caught her on his way out and pulled her into his arms.

"It's okay," Dylan said. "Everything's in place. There's no sign that he's been inside the house. Do you have Sukey's phone number?"

"No, but I can get it from Alma."

"Do it and then call Sukey and see if the flowers were here when she cleaned."

"Maybe they were delivered while she was here," Collette said. "If he delivered them himself, she could have seen him."

"Don't count on that."

"We're past due for a break." She called Alma on her cell phone, interrupting a pedicure. A few minutes later she had Sukey on the phone.

"The house looks great," Collette said, not wanting to alarm her.

"Thank you. I dropped your key off with Mrs. McGuire when I finished."

"Thanks. I'll get it from her." After a moment's hesitation she asked, "Did someone deliver flowers while you were here?"

"They were sitting by your door when I got there and were starting to wither. I put them in the vase of water for you and tied the pretty pink ribbon that held them around the vase. They looked better right away."

"Yes, they're lovely. I just thought you might have seen the man who delivered them."

"No, but whoever sent them must like you a lot. It's a really big bouquet."

Someone must really like her, all right. They'd like her dead. They must also think she was a moron.

She disconnected the call after thanking the woman again, then turned to Dylan. "Could this man possibly be so arrogant that he believes a bouquet of flowers will make me think he's not the man who attacked Eleanor?"

"You wouldn't know it with such certainty if we hadn't discovered that the last call was made from the hospital. No reason for him to think he's not still calling with impunity."

"And free to roam the hospital conniving to get into Eleanor's room and kill her."

"Maybe not," Dylan said. "He may have found out that she's been talking to the sheriff and assumes she's already given a description of him. But we still need to move quickly."

"Agreed. I'll get my daily planner. We can work at my kitchen table. That will give us more room to spread out." Besides, she couldn't avoid the room forever just because it reminded her of the attack.

Dylan followed her down the narrow hallway and explained his plan. "I'll start going through the phone records and circle all the ones that could be from the stalker. Hopefully we'll find a pattern between his calling and where you'd been and who you'd seen on those days."

And if there was a pattern, that would at least give them a place to start. If the pattern involved a specific location—stores, banks, offices—the sheriff's department could confiscate the appropriate security footage and see if anyone appeared to be following her.

Success was iffy, as Dylan had said when he'd proposed his plan, but doing something was far better than waiting for the next vicious drama to unfold. Or for the results of the DNA testing.

A minute later she returned to the kitchen and set her planner on the table near Dylan's elbow. "I'm having a diet cola. Would you like one?"

"No, thanks, but water would be good," he said, circling in red another suspect call from the list of numbers.

She got him a glass of water and then pulled the soda from the fridge and popped the cap.

"Did you make note of the dates or times of

any of the stalker's calls?" Dylan asked as she slid into a chair next to his.

"I didn't the first few times, but I started keeping track of all of them about three weeks ago. I received the first call from him around the middle of March."

"How about March twelfth at ten-thirty in the evening?" Dylan asked. "That's the first indication I see of a call from a number that can't be traced to an individual account."

"The time sounds right. I know I was working late in my studio the first time he called."

She checked her calendar for that day. "I had a sitting with the Clerys for their adorable daughter's first-birthday pictures, a consultation with the Aldings of Marble Falls for an upcoming wedding, and I'd gone to Betts Cummings's real-estate office to photograph her at her desk for a new Web site she was having designed."

"You do stay busy."

"And I can't keep canceling appointments the way I've done this week. Let's see, there was also a late-afternoon dentist appointment for my semiannual cleaning."

She checked the date for the following weekend. The gallery showing was marked and highlighted in yellow.

"That could have well been the date of his first

call. I know I was framing some photos I'd taken of lightning bolts during a recent storm."

Dylan looked up from his list. "You take pictures of storms?"

"Sometimes. I'd been experimenting with various shutter speeds and that night I got it right. The clarity of the streaks of light was remarkable. One of the Austin galleries was having a big show that coming weekend and had asked to include some of my nature photographs so I was working extra late."

"I'd love to see some of your work."

"The first chance we get, as long as you promise to be duly impressed by my offerings."

"I can't imagine not being impressed by anything you do."

A preposterous burn crept to her cheeks. At twenty-seven, she shouldn't blush at a casual compliment. Had the comment come from anyone but Dylan, she'd have paid it no mind. This was just more of the sensually decadent effect he had on her. And reason enough to keep her mind on the task at hand.

"If I'd any idea the calls would lead to this, I would have kept excellent records. But who expects this kind of trouble in Mustang Run?" She realized as soon as the words were out of her mouth that Dylan was not the person to have said that to, not after what had happened to his mother in this town. And that had been when the population was much smaller than it was now.

"Nowhere is totally safe these days," Dylan said. "If someone's motivated to commit crimes, they find a way."

Motivation was the key. What was the motivation for stalking her or for wanting her dead?

"What about March eighteenth?" Dylan asked. "You received another suspicious call on that day, this one at 1:10 p.m."

She checked the calendar. "That was a Saturday. My to-do list says pick up nails to fix a loose shutter and meet Melinda and Eleanor in Austin for an early dinner."

"Where did you shop for nails?"

"At Knight's Hardware. It's just a couple of blocks from my studio." Her memory kicked in with a gasp of insight. "That's also where I got the bronzed metal paint for the frames I made for the lightning bolts. I stopped by there on my way back to the studio that night. Mr. Knight was just locking up, but he waited for me to purchase what I needed."

"How often do you visit Knight's Hardware?"

"Maybe once a month, but I pass it every time I walk down to Abby's or Joyce's Soups and Salads for lunch. That's at least a couple of times a week."

"Tell me about the employees at the hardware store."

"There's usually just Larry Knight, his nephew Kingsley and sometimes Larry's wife, Jane. Larry's the owner."

"What do you know about Larry?"

"Larry Knight is a family man, hardworking, active in his church and works with the Boy Scouts. I was photographing his son Carl's wedding the night Eleanor was attacked. Believe me, Larry has not been stalking me. Besides, I know his voice."

"What about Kingsley?"

"He's still in high school, a senior, I think. He only works part-time. He's always friendly and helpful when I go in, but he's never been into any trouble that I know of. Again, I know his voice and his cheerleader girlfriend. You can rule him out, too."

"Do they have security cameras inside the shop?"

"Probably inside and out. Everyone does these days, except me." She'd remedy that soon. Mustang Run was not as safe as she'd believed.

"I say we call your father and have him put someone on checking that footage."

"I doubt we have to wait on the sheriff's department. If we explain the situation to Larry, he'll probably hand over the disk to us, or at least let us view the footage. I'm sure he's already heard about Eleanor's attack, or at least some version of it."

"Then let's do it," Dylan said. "We can check out the rest of these numbers and dates later at the ranch."

At the ranch. So he assumed she was staying again. She'd vowed not to. But that was to keep him from getting involved with her problems, and he was already in neck deep. Besides, if she didn't go back to Willow Creek Ranch, there would be no chance of a repeat visit from his mother's ghost.

Not that she believed in ghosts, but just in case she was wrong and the house at Willow Creek Ranch really was haunted... Helene might be the only one who had a clue what was behind the stalker's madness.

"Let me pack a few more things."

Picking up her drink and her planner, she went back to the bedroom. She tossed a small overnight bag onto the bed and unzipped it. The first panties she pulled from the bureau were a pair of white briefs. Impulsively, she dropped them back to the stack and chose a lacy red thong and a black lace bikini panty.

She gathered some jeans and T-shirts and pulled out a pair of white shorts while she was at it. The weather was getting warmer, or at least she was.

Once everything was in the overnighter including her appointment book, she zipped the bag, slung it over her shoulder and stepped over to close the closet door.

She hesitated and then reached onto the top shelf of the closet and removed the plastic shoe box marked Personal. Opening the luggage again, she fit the box of letters inside. If she was already being haunted by ghosts, maybe it was time to let the secrets in her closet come out of hiding, too.

"NICE HORSES AND thoughtful of Bob Adkins to let you use them. I guess you'll find who your real friends are day by day."

"I suspect I can count them with the fingers of one hand." Troy scratched the nose of the flaxen chestnut filly who'd come to the pasture fence to check them out. "I didn't expect you to be among the number."

Ruthanne propped the heel of a stylish Western boot on the bottom rung of the recently repaired fence. "Helene was my best friend, Troy. I trusted you, as well. You know that. I was just too shocked and stunned by the murder to reason it all through back then."

"So you went with the tide of popular opinion and shunned me like the rest."

Which was why he'd been so surprised to see her at his door a few minutes earlier. He'd recognized her at once. In fact, she didn't look all that different than she had almost two decades ago. Ruthanne Foley had always been beautiful. She still was. Money had a way of softening the edges of a woman and keeping the wrinkles at bay.

She reached over and ran her fingers through the horse's thick mane. "I wanted to testify to your character at the trial, but Riley was dead set against it. He thought I was too close to the situation to see it clearly."

"He thought your befriending me would cost him votes." Troy had never been one to dance around the truth. "Does Riley know you're here now?"

"He doesn't know or care where I am anymore. We separated last year. He stays in Austin fulltime now. I moved back to the family ranch."

"Your choice or his?"

"The divorce or the ranch?"

"Either. Both."

"It was his choice to take a mistress, a blonde young enough to be his daughter, all very clandestine, of course. It was my choice to leave him and move back to the ranch."

"How are the kids?"

"Marilyn's teaching kindergarten and living at the ranch with me. Ellie is modeling in New York. She's the one I worry about. I heard Dylan is here with you."

"For the time being."

"I also heard that he's gotten mixed up in some trouble involving Collette McGuire."

Troy's muscles grew taut. "He and Collette are old friends. He's doing what he can to help her."

"That's not the way Glenn sees it."

Glenn. He took that to mean they were close enough that her information had come straight from the sheriff's mouth. "You got something on your mind, just say it, Ruthanne. If I ever had the knack for small talk, I lost it in prison."

"There's no love lost between Glenn and you, Troy. You know that. You'd best warn Dylan to watch his step very carefully."

"Is that what you stopped by to tell me?"

Ruthanne put her hand on his arm and leaned in so close he could see the rise of her breasts inside her white shirt and feel her silky black hair against his flesh.

A slow burn crept though him. It had been eighteen years since he'd been with a woman, and he was human. Too human. But even if she was offering, he couldn't be with Ruthanne without thinking of Helene.

And the ache inside him for Helene would be too devastating to let him even go through the motions. He had to have some kind of closure first, had to get justice for Helene. Then maybe he could move on, but he would never stop loving her.

"I need to get back to work," he said.

"Is that my signal to disappear?"

"If you've finished saying what you came to say."

"I've finished. But take my warning seriously. If Glenn can find a way to run Dylan out of town and away from Collette, you can be sure he will."

"Right, and you can tell the sheriff for me that I will not stand by and let him railroad my son the way he did me."

"I'll be sure he gets the word. If you want to talk some night, call me. I'd like that."

"I expect to be busy for a long time."

DYLAN WAS RELIEVED that Larry Knight had been eager to help. He not only provided the disks containing the security-camera footage for both days, but let them use his office and both his laptop and desktop computers to view them. His wife had even brought in bottles of water and cups of coffee.

Dylan chose the footage for March 12. In the desktop he loaded the disk from the camera closest to the front door. He put the one that scanned aisles beyond the checkout counter into the laptop. He fast-forwarded both files to just before six o'clock, Larry's usual closing time.

One man checked out at five minutes before six. Other than Larry Knight, he appeared to be the only person in the shop. Kingsley was either not working or was in the back.

"The man checking out is Skip Wakefield, the principal of the high school," Collette noted. "He's short and I can probably bench press more than him, so that pretty much rules him out as tall and muscled."

But Larry was both tall and muscled. Dylan decided not to mention that for now.

At two minutes before six, the film showed Collette walking through the door.

Larry smiled and motioned her to come in as she opened the door. Once she was inside, he took a key ring from his pocket and locked the front door.

"I think I asked if he was ready to close," she said.

"Obviously, he didn't want any additional customers."

"Probably not, though I have been in after the posted hours when he was still open for business. I think it all depends on what he has to do on a particular night."

"No sign of Kingsley tonight," Dylan commented. He'd hoped to see what the guy looked like. He might not be able to judge a book by its cover, but he could tell a lot about a guy by looking at him, especially if he could look the guy in the eyes.

Collette and Larry stepped out of view of one camera and into the view of the other. They were looking at small cans of paint.

"I wanted to give the frames an aged look," she said. "To do that, I distress the wood and use an antiquing rub. Larry stocks lots of different colors."

But Dylan's attention had moved to the other computer. A tall, muscled man wearing a T-shirt and faded jeans walked up to the door, tried it, but didn't move away when he discovered it was locked.

Instead he cupped his hand over his eyes and pressed his head to the glass as if he were trying to peer inside. He stayed a couple of minutes and then walked away. Dylan ran it back.

"Do you recognize this man?"

"No. I don't think I've ever seen him before.

But that means nothing. New people are moving into the area all the time."

"The timing is right for him to get to the door if he was following a half block or so behind you. Ask Larry to take a look at the film to see if he recognizes the man."

Dylan blew up the image and printed out two copies on the laser printer while Collette went for Larry. The printed images were a bit grainy, but clear enough.

Larry returned with Collette and studied the film. "I don't know him, but he looks vaguely familiar. He may have been here before. Let me get my wife and have her take a look."

Unfortunately, Mrs. Knight didn't recognize the man, either.

Dylan switched files to March 18. At 11:43 in the morning, Collette entered the store and went straight to the shelf where nails were stocked.

Exactly three minutes later, the man whose image he'd printed walked into the store. He stopped at the same aisle as Collette and looked—or pretended to look—at a display of electric screwdrivers. More than once his gaze scanned the aisle in Collette's direction. At one point he looked directly into the nearby camera and then quickly moved out of view.

Dylan got that buzz in his veins he used to get in Iraq when they were about to close in on the enemy. His gut instinct was that he was looking at Collette's stalker.

The film showed Collette leaving a few minutes later with her nails. Shortly thereafter, the guy walked out. He was not carrying a bag.

Dylan hadn't realized Collette had clued in on his suspicions until he felt her fingers digging into his arm.

"You think that's *him,* don't you?" she asked.

"I think it could be."

"If it is, then I don't think this was ever about his lusting after me or thinking I was his soul mate."

"Why is that?"

She shuddered. "The way he looked at me. Go back and run that part again. Only this time enlarge his face."

Dylan did. Even in black and white, the man's stare was cold and calculating.

"I think he's planned to kill me all along."

COLLETTE CALLED her father's cell-phone number on the way back to the ranch and left a message for him to call her. The sooner they got this picture in his hands, the sooner he could run a search and see if the man had a mug shot on record. She realized that could take a while. Everything seemed to take too long.

"Do you think your father has been home alone

all day?" Collette asked once they were inside the gate of Willow Creek Ranch.

"Yes, but I don't think he minds it. I think he may need the time alone to adjust to freedom and to come to grips with the past."

"It must be heartbreaking for him," Collette said. "Before the murder, he had a working ranch, a beautiful wife and five young sons."

"Now he just has empty pastures, rundown outbuildings, worn equipment and me," Dylan said, finishing her topic for her, though not in her words.

"He's lucky to have you, Dylan. And your brothers will come around. It just takes time."

"I know why I think he couldn't kill Mom, but what makes you so convinced he's innocent when a jury declared him guilty?"

Because I've talked to Helene.

Collette didn't dare say that out loud. She knew that Dylan would think her ghostly encounter was a nightmare or a hallucination. She thought so herself. She just wasn't as sure of it as she'd been before she'd seen and talked to Helene's ghost.

But that wasn't the only thing that convinced her of Troy's innocence. "When your father talked of your mother's garden, I could hear the grief and melancholy in his voice. He loved your mother. You don't destroy the person who holds your heart."

"My mother's side of the family was convinced that he did."

"What about your dad's family?"

"There is none. His mother died when he was a baby. His biological father had cut out long before that. He was raised in a series of foster homes. That's all I know about it. We were never encouraged to talk about our father once my grandparents had removed us from the ranch."

"They'd lost their daughter. Grief can instill the need for revenge at all costs."

Who knew that better than Collette? And Helene.

They topped the last hill and the Ledger ranch house came into view. The sheriff's vehicle and one additional squad car blocked the driveway. Her brother Bill's car was parked behind them. They wouldn't be out here for her, not after she'd refused to go with them last night.

Panic struck like one of her lightning bolts. "They must be here about Eleanor. The stalker must have found a way to get to her."

Dylan reached for her hand and squeezed it. "You don't know that."

"Why else would everyone be here except to deliver the bad news?"

She jumped from the car the second Dylan stopped, and raced toward her father's car. He was standing beside it when she reached him.

The look on his face was grim. One hand rested on the mirror of the car, the other on the butt of the pistol at his waist.

"Please tell me Eleanor is okay."

"Eleanor's fine," he sputtered. "Why wouldn't she be? She's under protective custody."

Dylan had walked up behind her, his presence calming her in spite of her father's callous attitude.

"Then why are you here?" Dylan asked.

"To see you and to give you a ride down to my office." He opened the back door of his squad car. "Get in."

Chapter Fourteen

Dylan needed a minute to think, but the situation was fast barreling out of control. Collette was livid and in the sheriff's face letting him know about it. A horse neighed in the distance. There was no sign of his father, but Dylan was certain he'd show up and join the circus at any minute.

"What reason do you have for taking Dylan in?" Collette protested. "He told you everything he knew right after the attack."

"He's a person of interest. Now get your things and Bill will drive you to his house. This lame-brain game you're playing with Dylan Ledger has gone on long enough."

"I'm not playing games. I'm as aware as anyone how serious this is. That doesn't give you the right to harass Dylan."

"This is law business, Collette, and none of your affair."

"So let's just get the show on the road," Dylan said, not wanting to pit Collette against her father any longer. "Go with your brother, Collette. I'll call you as soon as the sheriff finishes the *law business*."

"I'm not going anywhere. I'll be waiting right here when you return."

"No daughter of mine is staying alone in a house with a convicted killer."

The sheriff was pushing it now. Dylan had to fight the anger that swelled inside him. He might have to settle things with the sheriff one day, but right now his total focus had to be on keeping Collette safe, and he couldn't do that from a jail cell.

Dylan put an arm around Collette's shoulders, knowing that would irritate her father even more, but he couldn't leave her without some kind of assurance.

"I'll be fine. The sooner I talk to the sheriff about the evidence we discovered this afternoon, the sooner he can follow up on it."

The sheriff narrowed his eyes and glared at Dylan. "What evidence is that?"

"We checked out security footage from the hardware store and we think we may have spotted Collette's stalker."

McGuire turned back to Collette. "Is he talking straight?"

"Yes. The man on camera appeared to be following me on two different occasions on days that corresponded with the first two phone calls I received. We printed out his picture."

The situation was beginning to diffuse when Dylan spotted Troy walking back from the horse barn. Troy picked up his pace when he spotted the squad cars, his shoulders squared and his gaunt face looking as if he was about to climb in the ring with a killer.

Dylan had no idea what his father was capable of when he was fighting mad, but he figured they were about to find out.

"What's going on here?" Troy demanded.

"No problem, Dad," Dylan said, hoping to keep Troy out of this. "The sheriff just wants me to come in and answer a few more questions about the attack."

Troy's body clenched as if he was about to explode. "Do you have a warrant?"

"No," McGuire said. "He's not under arrest. He's just a person of interest."

Troy bristled. "Same as I was, Glenn, when you framed me?"

"Don't ride that road, Troy, not if you expect to come back and live in this town."

"You don't own the town. And there's nothing you can do to me that's near as bad as what's already been done. But I won't sit back while you railroad my boy. He'll talk when there's an attorney present and not before. I've already hired one."

Dylan had the good sense to realize this was no longer about him. The enmity between Glenn McGuire and Troy Ledger was rooted in the past. Theirs was a fight that was probably long overdue.

But Dylan was his own man. "I'm going with the sheriff. I have information he needs."

"Information that Dylan and I spent the day tracking down," Collette threw in. "I'm staying here until Dylan returns. If you're worried about my being here without him, Dad, then I suggest you make the questioning session short. And then get on with finding the stalker."

"Do as you please." McGuire was so furious his mouth could barely form the words. He turned his back on his daughter and got into his squad car.

The sheriff had won the battle he'd come here to fight, but he may have lost the war with Collette.

DYLAN HAD BEEN GONE for just over an hour when Collette picked up the dreaded stack of letters her mother had given her and walked to the weeds, briars and thorns that had once been Helene's beloved garden.

After being shot at on the porch the other

night, she didn't trust any outside area open to sniper fire. Tucked between the stone wall and two added extensions of the meandering ranch house, the garden felt safe and protected. On the other hand, the letters she held felt like explosive contraband.

Using a tissue from her pocket she brushed leaves and dirt from the rusting metal bench and dropped onto it. Nothing she held in her hand would bring her mother back. Yet the yellowed letters that had stayed in the top of Collette's closet for years without notice were suddenly begging to be opened and have their secrets revealed.

The larger envelopes were all addressed to Helene Martin.

Collette's chest constricted painfully as she stared at the name. Helene Martin, Dylan's mother. Surely her father had not been involved with Helene. Her hands began to shake, and she struggled with a wave of nausea.

Below the stack of letters, one note-size square envelope was addressed to Glenn McGuire in neat, precise penmanship. Dread eating away at her, Collette opened it first, took a deep breath and started reading.

Dear Glenn,
Please do not write me again as it is time

for both of us to move on with our lives. I never meant to lead you on. We had great times together, but it wasn't love, at least not for me.

I know you feel that both Troy and I have betrayed you since he was your friend long before you introduced him to me. But if you must blame someone, blame me. It was I who pursued him.

I love Troy with all my heart, and I know that he loves me, too. We're getting married in May, as soon as graduation is behind me. I am returning your letters so that you can destroy them and put that part of your life behind you.

I wish you all the best in life and hope that one day you and Troy can be friends again. I know he would like that.
Warmly,
Helene

Collette trembled as full awareness of what she'd just read seared into her mind. That friendship had clearly never come to be. But had the perceived betrayal led to her father framing Troy Ledger for Helene's murder while he let the real killer go free? Nagging suspicions ground in the back of Collette's mind. She had to know the truth.

An unexpected chill settled deep inside her as she reread the letter, and she had the eerie sensation that she was no longer alone in the garden. Could it be that Helene was reading over her shoulder? Oddly, the possibility did not disturb her.

She read the rest of the letters one by one, feeling her father's loss, yet hurting for her mother. She could imagine her mother's heart breaking at the vows of love Glenn McGuire had written to another woman mere months before they were married. Tears burned and filled Collette's eyes until she could barely make out the words.

The letters were full of the angst her father was experiencing, but they were also informative enough to give her an idea of the circumstances surrounding his breakup with Helene.

Her father had also been a senior at UT at the time. Apparently he and Helene Martin had been dating for over a year when Glenn brought her home with him for the weekend. He'd introduced to her his best friend, wild and reckless Troy Ledger, a cowboy who hadn't gone to college and who was riding the rodeo circuit and saving every cent of his winnings to buy his own spread. That trip was the beginning of the end for Glenn and Helene and the beginning for Troy and Helene.

There was not one mention of Collette's mother in the letters, though judging from the dates,

Glenn must have turned to Mildred during this time. No wonder Collette's mother had been so hurt when she read them. She became pregnant with Glenn's child while he had been touting his love for another woman and begging her to take him back.

And yet Collette's parents had made a life together—until a frayed stack of yellowed letters and a tragedy had ended it.

Footsteps on the old stone walkway startled Collette. This time the visitor was flesh and blood.

"I cooked some stew," Troy said, staring at her red-rimmed eyes, but not asking her what was wrong. "I can't vouch for its quality, but food with any flavor tastes like gourmet to me."

"I should have offered to help," she said.

"You're a guest."

"Some might say an intruder," Collette countered.

Troy didn't argue the point. He was surely no more enamored of her relationship with Dylan than her father was, albeit for different reasons.

"I'm sorry my father is being so hard-nosed about this," she said, hoping to smooth the moment.

Troy didn't respond, but she could see his features harden.

"If the sheriff has issues with me, he should take them up with me, not with my son."

"I agree, but I can't speak for my father."

"Right, so let's just drop that subject. Now what's this about new information that you and Dylan tracked down?"

Collette explained the findings. "I think all of the talk of love and soul mates may have been a ruse. I think the stalker's real motives may stem from something else."

"Did he try to blackmail you?" Troy asked.

"No. He just seemed to delight in upsetting me. I think he could be seeking revenge."

"Who would have that kind of grudge against you?"

"I think the grudge may be against my father." Even now in the garden haunted by Helene, Collette didn't mention that the ghost of Troy's dead wife had put her on that track. She definitely didn't mention the letters she'd just read.

"I suspect there are lots of people with grudges against your father." Troy reached down and pulled one weed from the multitude that clogged the beds. "I should get this area in shape. Helene would hate seeing it this way. She liked pretty things. I provided so few, but she never complained. She claimed she didn't need trinkets or luxury to be…"

A gravelly quake in his voice swallowed the

last of his words. Coming home to life without Helene was clearly tearing him apart. "She had you and the boys," Collette said. "That's worth far more than inanimate possessions."

"Her parents never saw it that way. They wanted her back in Boston to be part of the elite circles they moved in. They wanted her to have expensive clothes and jewels and to send the boys to private schools."

"If Helene's family was from Boston, how did Helene end up at the University of Texas?"

"She was a bit rebellious, wanted to live where it was warm and she liked cowboys." Finally, Troy smiled, deepening the creases around his eyes. "The real miracle is that she ended up with me."

"The miracle was love."

A love so strong that all these years later Collette could still feel it in this garden. Feel it as surely as she could feel the breeze that tousled her hair and danced across her cheeks.

She'd never really believed in that kind of love before. Now that she knew it existed, she wanted it. She could see herself having it with Dylan.

But Dylan could never love a woman whose father had been instrumental in sending the only parent he had left to prison for a crime he didn't commit.

DANGER WAS IMMINENT. The reality of that echoed in Dylan's mind as he stepped from the deputy's car and walked toward the ranch house. He had a sixth sense about looming disaster. It had saved his life more than once in Iraq.

Like the time he'd been leading his squad into a trap. At the last minute his instincts for pending catastrophe had forced him to pull back. Only later had they discovered how close they'd come to being blown to bits.

This time the fear was for Collette, and he had more than his gut feeling to rely on. He had the land mines she'd narrowly missed.

She'd missed being attacked and likely killed the other night by a matter of minutes—possibly because he'd stopped by her house on an impulse. She'd missed having her brains splattered over the porch by a matter of inches. The man who was masterminding the situation with claims of infatuation and gifts of flowers wanted Collette dead. There was no reason to think he wouldn't strike again.

If Dylan was going to keep her safe, he had to stay out of jail himself. The sheriff had other ideas, and his reason for wanting to discredit Dylan was clear: for protection Collette had chosen the "murderer's kid" over her sheriff father.

Yet McGuire had taken the photo from the

security-camera footage, and Dylan was sure he'd check it out. The man was vindictive to a fault, but he wanted his daughter safe.

Troy was waiting on him in the kitchen when Dylan walked in. A sheaf of papers was sitting on the table in front of him.

"How'd it go?" Troy asked.

"In redundant circles."

"That's McGuire's way of trying to trip you up."

"I don't trip," Dylan said, "and the sheriff doesn't have a shred of evidence against me. He just wants me out of Collette's life."

Troy pushed his chair back from the table. "It is strange that Collette's turned to you when she hardly knows you."

Dylan had no answer for that. All he knew was that he and Collette had connected instantaneously from some kind of uncanny chemistry that defied reason. And right now he couldn't wait to see her again. "Has Collette gone to bed?"

"She went to her room after dinner. I saved you some stew. I'll heat it for you while you take a look at those printouts."

Dylan scanned what looked like articles downloaded from the computer. Surely Troy hadn't left Collette here alone and unprotected while he went somewhere to get on the Internet.

"Where did you get these?"

"My friend Able Drake looked it all up for me. He forwarded it to Bob Adkins who was nice enough to print it out and run it over to me."

"You've been busy while I've been out."

"Collette suggested the stalker's motivation could be a grudge against her father," Troy said. "That makes sense to me. These are names of people and reasons why they might seek payback against McGuire."

Seeing Collette would have to wait a few more minutes. Dylan had to read the articles. "Thanks, Dad. And the stew sounds good."

He dropped to the chair and started reading, making note of the people who looked the most suspicious. Billy Sikes topped the list. He'd been arrested ten years ago for running a car-theft ring, stripping the vehicles and selling the parts. He'd been released from jail this past January and arrested again in March for robbing a liquor store. He was now out on bail and claiming that he was being framed by McGuire.

Alan Riggins was also suspect. He'd been accused of stalking the daughter of one of McGuire's deputies. He'd been nonfatally shot by said deputy. He'd filed charges against the deputy and the sheriff, saying McGuire had covered for the deputy, calling it self-defense when it was a clear case of police brutality. The deputy and the sheriff were cleared of all charges.

Then there was the case of Fancy Granger. The sheriff's office had been called by a neighbor to settle a domestic dispute in the mobile home Fancy shared with her live-in boyfriend. The anonymous neighbor reported screaming and feared the argument had grown violent.

Sheriff McGuire took the call along with one deputy. When he tried to arrest the boyfriend who was high on cocaine, Fancy Granger, also stoned, had pulled a gun on the sheriff. Gunfire had ensued, and Fancy Granger had been killed.

Dylan continued down the list. Eighty percent of the people in the county might love Glenn McGuire for being tough on crime, but he definitely had his share of enemies, especially among the criminal population.

He talked of the suspects with his father while he finished off the stew. His father was clearly concerned about him and willing to go to a lot trouble and the expense of hiring an attorney when his funds had to be extremely limited.

All of this now that Dylan was an adult. Yet he'd never once contacted Dylan or his brothers when they were growing up without him.

No excuse would satisfy Dylan, but still he needed to hear some kind of explanation for why Troy had denied him all those years.

He stood up and carried his bowl to the sink. "Why didn't you ever answer my letters?"

Troy twisted around in his chair. "What are you talking about? I answered all your letters, all nine of them. I wrote you and your brothers every week for years until Wyatt wrote and told me that none of you ever wanted to hear from me again."

"I never received a letter from you. Not one, Dad. Not one. Neither did Wyatt or any of the rest of us."

Troy banged his right fist into his left palm, over and over, as if he were kneading bread with his knuckles. "I wrote, son. The letters were mailed to your grandparents every week. I never knew you didn't receive them."

"Why would you mail the letters to them? Only one of us ever lived with them after the trial."

"I was under court order to go through them anytime I corresponded with any of you. I even tried to call whenever I had phone privileges. They never allowed me to speak to you. They said you didn't want to talk to me."

Troy walked over and put an arm about Dylan's shoulder. "I'm sorry, son. I should have pressed for more information. I should have tried harder. But your grandparents were right. I really didn't have anything to offer you but grief."

"They weren't right," Dylan said. "We lost Mother. We were kids. We needed our dad."

"I failed you. I'm sorry. I don't know anything else to say."

There was actually nothing to say. The hurt was still buried deep inside him. He'd missed his mother so much, he'd wanted to die. And then when he hadn't heard from his father, he'd felt lost and betrayed. He'd tried so hard to be strong. He never had been.

Maybe that's the real reason he'd joined the army, from a need to prove himself a man when he ached for the boy he'd never gotten to be.

"I'm sorry, Dylan. I kept up with you. I kept up with all of you. I knew when you graduated college and when you joined the army. I prayed for you every day. But I let you down. I should have found a way to get past your grandparents."

"You should have." He stared at his father, part of him wanting to lash out at him for not being the father he'd needed. Lashing out wouldn't change anything.

To get past this would take time. Yet for the first time in eighteen years, Dylan believed he and his father would find a way to be a family. He gave his father a hug, one that felt as if they were reaching across a huge gulf. Bridging it would be hard, but for now, this was enough.

"I wish we could start over, Dylan, but now is all I can offer."

"It's okay, Dad. It helps to know you tried. It doesn't erase the pain, but it helps. We'll get there in time, but right now we should probably get some sleep."

But instead of going to bed, Dylan went in search of Collette.

COLLETTE HAD JUST STEPPED from the shower when she heard the soft tapping at her door.

"Are you decent?"

Dylan. Her pulse quickened at the sound of his voice. She quickly pulled on her robe and then grabbed a towel to turban around her dripping hair.

"Come in."

He stepped through the door. Fatigue had settled in his broad shoulders. Her first impulse was to step into his arms, but knowing what she had to tell him held her back.

"Was the interrogation tedious beyond endurance?" she asked.

"Let's just say I'm not your father's favorite citizen. We Ledgers have a fearsome reputation."

And a history of trouble that started with the sheriff long before Helene's murder. "How did Dad react to the photo taken from the security footage?"

"He reminded me I'm not an officer of the law and have no business requesting security-camera evidence." Dylan mocked her father's stern tone.

She smiled in spite of the anxiety that was pulsing inside her. "Does nothing drag you into despair, Dylan Ledger?"

"The Cowboys losing a playoff game."

"You grew up in Boston."

"But I was born a Texan." He sat on the edge of the bed. "However, I get the feeling that something is bothering you."

She walked to the dresser, reached into the top drawer and removed the telltale correspondence. "I read the letters Mother gave me."

He took her hand and tugged her down beside him. "Do you want to talk about it?"

"I think I should."

His hand roamed her back. "Only if you want to."

"They could affect you, too."

He looked at her questioningly. She dreaded hitting him with this tonight, but with all her father was throwing at him, he deserved to know the full truth.

She met his gaze, and the quake inside her shook her control. "The woman my father was in love with when he married my mother was

Helene Martin." She pressed the handwritten note into Dylan's hand.

He winced as he started reading. By the time he was finished, his shoulders were squared, his back ramrod straight.

"I know what you're thinking, Dylan. I had the same thoughts, but nothing in those letters proves or even suggests that my father misused his power as sheriff when he arrested Troy."

"When my father went to prison, it didn't just steal seventeen years of his life, Collette. It ripped me and my brothers from him, from our home and from each other. Losing our mother broke our hearts. Losing our father as well destroyed our childhood and life as we knew it."

"I know. I'm so sorry." Tears burned her eyes. She stood and walked away from the bed.

"I don't blame you for any of this," Dylan said, "but if I learn that Glenn McGuire framed my father for murder because of a college crush he had on my mother, I'll find a way to make him pay, Collette. I couldn't live with myself if I didn't."

"I understand." Tears slid from her eyes and ran down her cheeks. "I'm not even sure I can ever forgive him for robbing my mother of the love she deserved. I know I have to talk to him face-to-face."

"When this is over."

"No, Dylan. I can't wait that long. I'm going to his house first thing in the morning."

"I can't see him confessing to anything."

"But I'll know," she said. "If I'm there, looking him in the eye, I'll know if he's lying."

"What a disgusting web this has become," Dylan said. "I thought I'd seen the worst of what life could throw at me when I was a kid and then again in Iraq. But it just keeps coming."

"Coming to my rescue certainly didn't help you."

Dylan crossed the room to where Collette stood staring out the window. He wrapped his arms around her and pulled her back to his chest. "This isn't our doing, Collette."

"Yet we're entangled in it."

Dylan's lips pressed into her neck, and the heat from the kiss sank deep inside her. But she couldn't give in to the need for him that swelled inside her, not when so much anguish was pushing them apart.

"Tell me about you," she said, pulling away.

"There's nothing to tell. What you see is what you get."

"How did you earn your medal?"

"Does that matter?"

"I need to concentrate on something besides the family mess that we're in."

"Fair enough." He went back to the bed and

perched on the edge, his left hand circling the bedpost. "We were on a search-and-rescue mission in a small Iraqi village where an earlier battle had gone bad.

"We got trapped by the enemy and had to pull back and wait for more tanks and firepower. We were pretty much secure for the time being when a mother came running from a house shouting that her little girl had been hit by gunfire and begging someone to help."

"Was she bait to lure you into danger?"

"We couldn't tell, but when she got hit by a rain of bullets from her own people, she just kept yelling for someone to save her daughter."

Dylan averted his gaze, staring at the wall. "To make a long story short, I got what coverage I could get from my guys, went into that bombed-out house and carried the daughter to safety. While I was there, I found three American Marines in the wreckage, injured but still alive. By some miracle outside my doing, I got them out and back behind our lines."

Dylan was so much a man. He never saw himself as a hero. She'd never see him any other way. Her heart was so full of Dylan Ledger right now that she could barely breathe.

She walked over, stepped in front of him and put her arms around his neck, pulling his face into the cushion of her breasts. "I can see now why you're so tough."

"That didn't make me tough, Collette. It made me human."

He stood and tugged the towel from her head, letting her damp hair hang free. "Tough would be offering to walk away from you right now."

She loosened the belt of her robe and let it slide off her shoulders, leaving her standing naked in front of him.

"Let's go for human."

Chapter Fifteen

Dylan rocked back on his heels, crazy with the need roaring inside him. If he acted on his instincts now, he'd pick up Collette, throw her onto the bed and ravage every inch of her. And likely scare her away for good.

He had to take this slow. Savor every delicious touch. Pleasure Collette until she ached to feel him inside her with the same rampant, agonizing hunger he was feeling now.

He cupped her beautiful breasts, letting his thumbs pebble the nipples until they were hard and erect. He wrapped his lips around one, sucking gently and teasing with his tongue. She moaned softly and arched toward him. His erection grew so hard he thought it might burst from the worn denim.

When he reached down to unzip his jeans Collette's fingers intertwined with his. She reached her hand inside his briefs and slid her finger around the wet tip of his burgeoning staff. His control was losing steam. The rest of him was hotter than an explosion.

Still, he held back. His first time with Collette had to be as near perfect as he could make it for her. It struck him then that he'd never felt this way about a woman before. Never thought about the future and that he wanted her not just now, but time after time, day after day.

That should scare him. It didn't. His brain was numb with desire.

She stroked him as he shucked his jeans and shrugged out of his shirt. Passion engorged him and sent blood rushing to his already raging erection. He fell back on the bed, tugging Collette with him as they stretched across the crisp, white sheets.

The sight of her naked body bathed in the filtered shimmer of moonlight touched his soul. The sweet, salty taste of her lips as he took her mouth with his set him on fire.

"You're the one thing I never expected to find in Mustang Run," he whispered as they came up for air.

"Is that what took you so long to get here?"

He didn't answer. He was too lost in the primal cravings that throbbed in his body and deadened his mind.

COLLETTE CLOSED HER EYES, afraid to open them even to look at the enthralling hunk of a man who was touching her in the most private of places and sending spikes of pleasure deep into her core. She'd been intimate with men before. She'd never made love like this, never had a raw hunger for anyone possess her this completely.

She trailed her hand down the length of Dylan's erection. He captured her hand with his and slipped them both between her legs so that she felt her own slick heat. The uninhibited sharing of their bodies made her want him that much more, and when he lifted himself to straddle her, her heart began to pound like a primitive drum.

Dylan put his mouth to her ear, nibbling and sucking her ear lobe. "Guide me in, baby. Make me yours."

She'd never wanted anything more.

Wrapping her hand around the hard length of him, she led him to her, holding her breath until she felt him thrust deep inside her. Exhilaration vibrated through her, sending her pulse skyrocketing and creating a river that flowed from her core with liquid fire.

Dylan's thrusts became a crescendo, the rhythm building until there was no holding back. He rocked her with him as she exploded into an orgasm so intense she thought her heart might burst free of her body.

Only then did she feel Dylan let go of the tight rein he'd held on his body. Calling her name, he let the orgasm overtake him, his erection throbbing within her. She milked him with her hips, drawing out every last drop of pleasure. Reveling in the moment, she let her hands trail down his back to his buttocks, memorizing every muscle and sinew.

Moments later, Dylan rolled over and pulled her into his arms. But even as the golden symphony of afterglow began to hum through her, it was still difficult to breathe.

The words *I love you* echoed in her mind, though she didn't dare say them out loud. She shouldn't even think them this soon, but she knew they were true. Maybe a woman always knew.

The euphoria wouldn't lessen the problems that waited for them at the first light of morning. But for now, she found heaven here in Dylan's arms, and no matter what the future brought, she'd hold these memories for the rest of her life.

MORNING CAME TOO SOON and even the sweet ache in Collette's thighs wasn't enough to ward off the anxiety about facing her father with the letters and accusations.

"You could still wait to do this," Dylan said, as he followed her directions to the small house her father had moved into after his wife's death. "Confronting the sheriff might be easier on you after the stalker is behind bars."

"I'd consider postponing the inevitable if Dad wasn't trying to run my life and ruin yours."

"Don't make me the issue here, Collette. This is between you and him. I have my own issues with your father, but I'll deal with them my way when the time is right and I have all the facts."

"I just want an explanation. I know it won't change anything, but I have to brazen out the confusion."

"Don't expect too much," Dylan said. "Men don't always grasp all the emotional implications the way women do."

"I don't expect a defining resolution, but I deserve to know if he ever loved my mother or if he destroyed her for the sake of some cruel charade."

"Do you want me to go in with you?"

"No. I have to face him alone. The house is on the right, second one from the end of the block."

"I don't see his car," Dylan said.

"He parks it in the garage."

She reached for the door handle as Dylan stopped in front of the two-bedroom brick in one of Mustang Run's older subdivisions. Dylan reached across the seat, put his arm around her shoulder and pulled her close for a kiss. It was tempered with restraint but still she felt the impact curl around her heart.

He brushed a lock of curls from her forehead. "Good luck."

"Thanks."

She marched up the walkway, her fingers clutching the strap of the handbag that held the letters. She pushed the doorbell twice and waited. Seconds later she pushed it again.

"Hold your horses," her father shouted. He was barefoot and buttoning his shirt when he opened the door. "Look who's here and dying to get in." He stood back for her to enter. "Come to your senses, did you?"

"I came to talk."

"If it's to convince me Dylan is an innocent saint, you can save your breath. I have no use for the Ledgers. Never have. Never will."

"And now I know why." She unzipped her handbag and took out the letters.

Her father bent over for a better look, then staggered backward. "Where did you get those?"

"Mother gave them to me a few weeks before she tried to leave you."

He murmured a low curse and pressed his fingertips against both temples. "How in tarnation did she get her hands on those?"

"She found them in the attic, in an old chest of yours. The question is why did you keep them instead of destroying them?"

"Who knows why I did anything back in those

days? I was a know-it-all college student with a chip on my shoulder."

She wasn't convinced he'd changed all that much.

"There's no telling what was up in that attic," Glenn stammered. "None of it means anything anymore. Mildred, of all people, should have known that." He padded back to the living room, not seeming to notice or care if Collette followed him.

When she got there he'd dropped into his worn recliner and was cradling his head in his hands.

If he thought she was going to drop this, he was wrong. "Do you remember what you wrote in those letters to Helene Ledger?"

"I don't care what's in the damn letters. And she was Helene Martin back then. She wasn't married. Neither was I at the time I wrote them."

"But my mother was pregnant with Bill."

"From a stupid mistake one night when—"

Anger roared through her with such force she had to grip the back of the couch to hold steady. "Don't call my mother a mistake."

"I never have." His voice cracked. "The pregnancy was a mistake. I married Mildred. We made it right."

"But you were still in love with Helene."

Glenn threw his hands up in frustration. "I loved another woman thirty years ago, Collette. She dumped me for Troy Ledger. Is that what you want to hear?"

"No, I want to know if you ever loved my mother."

"How dare you ask me that?" Glenn raked his weathered fingers through his thinning hair. His eyes were moist, his lips pulled tight. "I loved your mother from the first day she laid that red, squalling brother of yours in my arms. She had to know that."

"How would she, Dad, when all you did was scowl and complain? When you constantly issued orders like a drill sergeant and made light of her wishes?"

"That's who I am. She knew that. I loved her. I didn't tell her enough, but she knew. She had to know." His shoulders shook. "If she'd only come to me with those stupid letters. If she'd only given me a chance to explain..." He dabbed at his eyes with the cuff of his shirt.

Seeing her father like this hurt more than Collette would have ever imagined. It was as if they were burying her mother all over again. She ached to go to him and tell him that she believed him, that in spite of all the antagonism of the past, she still loved him.

But the hurt went too deep to just sweep it

away like yesterday's dirt. And there was still the matter of Troy and Dylan Ledger.

Glenn stood and finished buttoning his shirt. "I'll burn the letters," he said, "the way I should have done thirty years ago. It's all I can do."

"I just have one more question," she said.

Finally he met her gaze straight on. "You seem to be the one in control here. Ask away."

She didn't need the control, not anymore. She'd learned more about her father in the past few minutes than she had in the twenty-seven years of her life. He was a blustering bear, but there was more to him. The tender and loving part of him was just hidden so deep inside that few people ever saw the real him. She prayed her mother had, for her sake and for his.

Unless…

The remaining question twisted inside her and tore at her heart.

"Did you frame Troy Ledger for his wife's murder?"

The transformation in her father was immediate and dramatic. His features hardened to granite. His eyes became a fiery storm.

"I put my life on the line any time it's needed in order to keep the citizens of this county safe, Collette. I don't back off from criminals, the politics or the media. I might have bent the strict restraints of the law from time to time, but by God,

I have never framed any man or woman to get a conviction."

"Not even a man you admit to hating?"

"I didn't have to. The evidence did that. A jury sent Troy Ledger to prison for brutally murdering his wife and the mother of his children. I would have given him a death sentence. Feel free to tell both Dylan and Troy that."

Her father turned and walked out of the room, leaving Collette to deal with his response any way she saw fit. She believed he was telling her the truth, but any chance of reconciliation between them would have to wait.

The would-be killer who spoke of love and soul mates but dealt in death wouldn't.

Chapter Sixteen

Tommy Jo Benoit stared out the window of his grandson's room on the third floor of Carlton-Hayes Regional Hospital and for the first time in his perverted life contemplated death. Forced to watch his eight-year-old grandson slowly lose his grip on life, Tommy Jo no longer saw death as a vague stagnation existing in grays and black, but as a predator who rode in on a blazing chariot in violent shades of red.

Tommy Jo would have gladly given his scarred, broken body and devil-owned soul to save the boy's life. But fate didn't bargain. Neither did the insurance company.

Now time was running out and Tommy Jo's well-laid plans were swirling down the toilet. When the clock was running down with the team behind and the time-outs depleted, someone had to come through with the game-winning play.

It didn't have to be pretty. It didn't have to be safe. It just had to work.

Tommy Jo reached beneath his jacket and touched his hand to the .45 resting in his shoulder holster. He'd made the deal. He'd see it through, though all the odds were against him now.

One life for another.

The pretty daughter of the sheriff would have to die.

Chapter Seventeen

The sixth floor was a din of clattering breakfast trays and rolling carts when Collette and Dylan stepped off the elevator.

"A new guard," Collette commented, as they neared Eleanor's room. "The nurses will be disappointed."

"He looks like he can handle the job to me."

"But he's not nearly as cute as the one on duty yesterday."

"I never noticed."

"I'd worry if you did."

Collette had been shaken and fighting tears when she'd climbed inside Dylan's truck after talking to her father. He'd let her talk, listening as he always did without passing judgment on her or her father. Though she still had a lot to sort through on that emotional front, Dylan had drastically improved her mood.

She had to admit now that it was possible that finding those letters had simply ignited a bout of insecurity in her mother, a meltdown that she would have recovered from without killing the marriage once she and Glenn had talked.

True, her parents hadn't had the kind of mutual esteem and equality in their union that Collette wanted, but that didn't mean it hadn't worked for them. She'd never know for sure, but it helped to realize that in his own way the domineering, stubborn and sometimes downright arrogant sheriff had loved his quiet and compliant wife. She just hoped her mother had found some happiness in the relationship, as well.

Eleanor's door opened and a man in a lab coat walked out followed by two nurses. Collette picked up her pace. "I hope that's just routine physician rounds and not a sign of complications."

"You'll find out soon enough," Dylan replied. "Did you mention to your father that you were planning to show Eleanor our hardware-store suspect's picture?"

"It didn't seem the ideal time for that. He doesn't like even a hint of us usurping his authority."

"As he made clear to me last night."

They stopped at the guard and Collette presented her ID.

"You're on the all-clear list," the guard told her.

"Does the patient have other company?"

"Melinda Kingston. She's on the list. Another guy stopped by here not ten minutes ago and tried to talk me into letting him in."

Collette felt a surge of apprehension and knew from the change in Dylan's stance that he felt it, too.

"Who was it?" Dylan asked.

"Some friend of the family. He left when I told him he wasn't on the list."

Collette pulled the photo from her handbag. "Is this the man?"

The guard studied it for a good half minute before handing it back to Collette. "No. The guy I talked to was ten to fifteen years younger than this man. But that guy in the picture looks familiar."

Dylan hooked his thumbs in the back pockets of his jeans. "Do you have any idea where you might have seen him before?"

"No, but I'll give it some thought. Check with me when you finish seeing Ms. Baker."

"I'll do that," Collette said. "But if you see him, don't let him near the patient."

"I'm not letting anyone near the patient unless they have proper ID and are on my list."

"Good man." Dylan turned to Collette and took her hand.

Even here, amidst all the trepidation and qualms, his touch both soothed and stirred her.

"Call me the second you leave Eleanor's room and I'll meet you here."

"Will do."

She slipped the picture back in her handbag and stepped into Room 612. This time Eleanor was sitting up in bed, sipping orange juice through a straw and watching a morning news show on the television.

Melinda was propped in a chair by the window. She jumped up and gave Collette a hug as they exchanged greetings. "Eleanor was just saying she hoped you'd stop by today."

"Can't keep me away." Collette walked to Eleanor's bedside. "You look a bit livelier than yesterday."

"They took that annoying IV out of my arm and I can actually go to the bathroom instead of using a bedpan. I'm sure those things should be outlawed as an inhumane form of torture."

Collette fluffed Eleanor's pillow. "Yep, you're on the road to recovery." Even her speech was clearer, though there were still enough meds in her to give her words a slight slur.

"A couple more days and I'll be ready to help your father go after the bastard who put me in the hospital," Eleanor said.

"How many times has Dad been up here to see you?"

"At least two that I was conscious for. Yesterday

right after you left and again in the afternoon. Thankfully, I could finally give him what he wanted."

"The articles?"

"No, I finally remembered the whole attack. Didn't he tell you?"

"As a matter of fact, he didn't. What did you remember?"

"That the attacker was wearing a mask, one of the rubber ones that kids wear at Halloween. It was hideously ugly, like some creature who'd come back from the dead and was covered in mud and blood. I guess that's why I'd blocked it from my mind."

Eleanor had described her attacker, and yet Collette's father hadn't mentioned that to her or to Dylan when he'd come calling at the ranch last night. If the man had been wearing a mask when he attacked Eleanor, then there was no way she could have recognized him, no way he'd need to come back to kill her.

So what was the stalker doing at the hospital?

Melinda reached for the remote and muted the television. "Your father is worried about you, too, Collette, especially with that strange alliance you've formed with Dylan Ledger."

Eleanor took the last sip of juice and set the empty carton back on her tray. "We're all worried about you, Collette. I mean, the guy chooses you out of dozens of reporters to invite into the Ledger house."

"You insisted I go in."

"Right, and don't think I don't regret that. But I didn't tell you to invite him to your house."

"I feel kind of responsible for all of this, too," Melinda said. "If I'd shown up to take the pictures, you'd have never been drawn into this or even talked to Dylan Ledger."

And now she'd made love to him and couldn't wait to do it again. Imagine what they'd think if they knew that.

"Dylan had nothing to do with the attack," she said, though she felt no real need to argue the point.

Eleanor rolled her eyes. "You, Collette McGuire, are much too naive."

Collette straightened Eleanor's sheet. "What did you tell Dad about Dylan?"

"I just voiced my concerns."

"Such as?"

"I received several threatening letters when I was investigating Helene Ledger's murder for a series of articles I was doing."

"What did the letters say specifically?"

"I don't remember specifically. Something about keeping my nose out of the murder if I wanted to die of natural causes. You know, the usual kind of threats investigative reporters get."

Fortunately, she didn't know. "I don't see how or why you'd connect those with Dylan."

"He could have been trying to protect his father."

"His father was already in prison for the murder," Collette reminded her.

"But he could have known the attorney was looking into a release based on a technicality."

"I didn't think investigative reporters gave credence to unproven hypotheses."

"Okay, I admit I have no idea who attacked me," Eleanor admitted. "I just think you should stay away from the Ledgers."

Not if Collette could help it, but there was no reason to try and reason with these two now. She slid the photograph from the outside pocket of her handbag and handed it to Eleanor.

"Have you ever seen this man before?"

Eleanor squinted and held the picture toward the light over her bed for a clearer view. "No. Should I have?"

"I think he could be my stalker." Collette passed the picture to Melinda. "How about you?"

"Never seen him before. Do you know his name?"

"Not yet. Dad's working on it, but for now he's what the cops on TV call an unsub."

Collette visited a few more minutes. When her cell phone vibrated, she checked the ID. It was her sister-in-law. She ignored the call for now and kept chatting with Melinda and Eleanor.

When Eleanor appeared to be growing tired, Collette said her goodbyes. Dylan wasn't waiting, so she decided to grab a diet soda and return Alma's phone call before calling him.

A nurse was chatting with a couple of visitors in the hallway outside Eleanor's room. She stopped talking long enough to point the way to the nearest refreshment room, which was just down the hall, not even out of sight of the guard on duty at Eleanor's room.

Collette retrieved her drink from the machine and was about to open it when the door to the room closed behind her. Before she knew what was going on, a large, misshapen hand covered her mouth and she was shoved against the drink machine.

"Finally we meet, my precious Collette."

DYLAN STEPPED into the first-floor coffee shop. He scanned the area, fully alert for any sign of the Hardware Stalker, as he'd come to think of him.

He picked up a black coffee to go at the

counter, paid for it and was about to leave when a woman at the back table turned in his direction and waved. It took a second before he realized it was Abby from the diner.

He walked over and sat down next to her. "I almost didn't recognize you without your floured apron."

"I get out of that kitchen every once in a blue moon. I'm not too keen on these hospital trips, though. They're too depressing. Just before you came in I was talking to a man whose grandson is dying from some rare disease that has no cure."

"That's rough."

She nodded. "Especially since the insurance company won't pay for some high-priced experimental drug that just might send the disease into remission. Poor guy. He said he was playing an option, though, and he was leaving to take care of it right then. Whatever that means."

"Hopefully it means the grandson will get the drug."

"The man looked familiar, but he said he'd never been in my diner. Claimed he'd never even driven though Mustang Run."

"I hope you told him he was missing out on the best coconut pie in all of Texas."

"Darn right I did."

"So what brings you to Carlton-Hayes?" Dylan asked.

"My neighbor had surgery last week. Not too serious. Got her gallbladder out, but she needed someone to drive her back for a checkup."

"And you're the Good Samaritan?"

She smiled at the compliment. "Better than hearing her whine about taxi fare. What brings you over from the ranch?"

"I drove Collette McGuire to visit a friend."

"Oh, yes. That friend who got attacked in her house, I bet. I heard you were the one who found her." Abby set down her cup and gave him a pat on the back. "Just returned to town and already the hero."

"I don't think calling an ambulance qualifies as heroic."

"I bet that's not what Collette is saying."

He got a strange buzz at the mention of Collette's name, partly from an anxiety that had grown steadily stronger since they'd walked into the hospital. His prelude-to-danger instinct was on high alert.

But he owed part of the buzz to the way Collette was burrowing inside him. Making love to her had been everything he'd imagined it would be, but instead of giving him release from the hunger that stirred at every touch, it only made the craving worse.

He wasn't sure if what he felt for her was love. In his lifetime he'd experienced lust and infatuation, but what he felt for Collette was on a whole new level. It would have to happen in the town where he'd always be known to some as the "murderer's kid" and with a woman whose father he might have to settle a score with one day soon.

If he was smart, he'd just leave town as soon as Collette was safe, before his heart got trampled into the hard Texas earth.

His cell phone rang. The caller was Sheriff McGuire. "Excuse me for a minute, Abby. This could be important." Or it could be more of the same garbage the sheriff had thrown at him last night.

"We've identified the man from Knight's Hardware," McGuire said as soon as Dylan answered. "He's got a rap sheet long enough he could use it for a blanket. Since you're supposedly protecting Collette, I thought you should know."

"I appreciate that. What's the full scoop?"

"His name is Tommy Jo Benoit. He was never prosecuted but he was a hit man twenty years ago for the Chicago mob. He fouled up a hit and the story is the mob messed him up real bad and put him out of the business for good. The Feds kept him under observation for years, but finally dropped him as a harmless has-been."

"How much damage did they do to him?"

"For starters they turned him into a steer."

"Ouch."

"They also fractured the bones in his gun hand and left him with iron plates in his head and screws in both arms. And they permanently damaged his vocal chords."

"Sounds like we've got our man."

"Closing in on him, anyway," Glenn admitted. "I've put out an APB on him. If he's still in the area, we'll get him. If he's not in the area, we'll still get him. It just might take a while longer."

"Thanks for the heads-up."

"Yeah. Good work on fleshing him out."

The compliment left Dylan dumbstruck.

"Take care of Collette," the sheriff said before breaking the connection.

That was a given.

Abby had finished her coffee by the time he put his phone away. She stood and then sat back down as if she'd just remembered something important. "Either that guy I was telling you about has a twin brother or he lied to me."

"What makes you think that?"

"I just remembered where I've seen him before—in my diner with Edna Granger."

Edna Granger. A local widow whose daughter was shot by McGuire. Alarm bells clamored in Dylan's brain. "Did the man happen to have an extraordinarily raspy voice?"

"Now how did you know that?"

The danger instincts had been right on target. Dylan took off in a dead heat with disaster.

COLLETTE STRUGGLED to free herself from the man's grasp until she felt the hard barrel of a pistol pressed into the base of her skull. "Make one sound and I pull the trigger."

The sandpaper voice was all too familiar. They wouldn't need to search for her stalker any longer. He'd found her.

She shivered, and cold sweat trickled down her face.

"Control yourself," he ordered. "We're going to take a short walk, Collette, just you and me. Two close friends in a hospital hallway. You will not do one thing to make anyone suspicious."

Adrenaline kicked in. So did hope. He wasn't going to shoot her here. She would find a way to escape.

He removed his hand from her mouth and let her turn so that she could see him. The gun remained lodged in the soft, fleshy spot beneath her brain.

Dylan had called it right. The stalker and the hardware suspect were one and the same. And now Dylan was somewhere inside the hospital, waiting on her to call the second she left Eleanor's room. Had she done that, she wouldn't be in this predicament.

But somehow this man would have found a way to get her. The cold, sick truth of that was in his eyes.

"Why are you doing this?" she asked him.

"No time for talk now. Just listen. I have six bullets in this gun, and I never miss my mark. Do anything to draw attention to us and the first bullet is for you. The rest are for innocent bystanders or fools who rush to your aid."

"You'll never get away with this. When the bullets are gone, they'll kill you."

"They did that twenty years ago," he whispered. "I have nothing to lose. So walk beside me quietly or you and five innocent bystanders will die. You're too noble and pure to let that happen, Collette."

"You know nothing about me."

"I know everything about you and about your lover. There will be no silver stars for Dylan Ledger this time. No chance to be a hero."

The man reached over and opened the door. "Now walk."

The short barrel of the pistol slid from the back of her head as he went through the doorway, marching her beside him into the hallway.

She didn't feel the gun now, but his arm was linked with hers, and she knew the gun was close at hand. She could take her chances if it was only her, but she couldn't risk his shooting innocent victims.

It could be a bluff, but she couldn't be sure. Mass murders of innocent victims had become all too frequent of late. She had to stay calm, search for a way to make a clean break, perhaps just as they reached the armed guard.

Only they turned and went in the opposite direction down the hallway. A nurse passed them and smiled. Collette kept walking, one step at a time, a psycho dressed in a nice sports shirt and creased khakis holding on to her arm with one hand, a gun in the other hand with a bullet carrying her name.

They turned a corner. An arrow and sign indicated they were heading toward the X-ray center. The glass doors ahead of them were marked for entrance by hospital personnel only. He surely wasn't a doctor. Someone would notice and call security. This would all be over soon.

Only he stopped before reaching the double doors, in front of another doorway marked Maintenance. The hallway remained empty as he pulled a key ring from his pocket and tried three keys before one fit, and the door opened.

The man was shrewd and collected, as if he did this sort of thing every day, as if he knew he wouldn't make a mistake. When the door opened, he shoved her inside and she nearly stumbled over a mop and pail. Her heart began to pound. Whatever this man wanted, he was not going to let her leave this room alive.

She lunged for him, tearing at his face with the fingernails of one hand as she went for his gun. He knocked her against the wall so hard that her brain seemed to rattle like a baby's toy. Acute pain shot up her shoulder and once more the barrel of the gun pressed against her flesh, this time at her right temple.

"I told you no games," he croaked.

Blood trickled from her mouth where she'd cracked it on the mop stick. She wiped it away with the sleeve of her cotton sweater. "Who are you? What do you want with me?"

"Right now I want you take off your clothes. All of them, but do it slowly so that I can get the full effect."

"Don't rape me," she pleaded. "Please, don't rape me."

He laughed, a growling vibration from deep in his throat. "If only I could. I told you. They killed me twenty years ago."

"Let me go," she pleaded.

"I said undress. Start with the sweater."

"No."

He laughed again. "No? You are a feisty one, aren't you?"

"If you want to kill me, do it, but I won't perform for you, you pervert."

Anger contorted his face and his eyes glazed over. "Very well, Collette. We'll do this the quick way. It's probably for the best anyway. Who knows when Dylan Ledger will come riding to your rescue and then I'd be forced to kill him, too. Not that I would find that offensive." He placed the gun on the shelf at his elbow while he pulled a pair of rubber gloves from his pocket.

It was now or never, she decided.

Instead of going for the gun, she reached for a bottle of bleach on the shelf beside her. In one quick motion she twisted off the cap and slung the bottle at him. Unfortunately, he ducked in time to miss the most of it.

He sputtered vile curses, but came at her with his eyes squinting from the caustic liquid. He pinned her against the wall, and his big hands closed hard around her neck.

"Thanks for the favor. I always preferred killing slowly with my bare hands so that I could watch the victim's faces as they realized they were dying. And you have such a pretty face, Collette."

She tried to fight him with her hands and feet, but her lungs were burning. She struggled for air.

"If it helps any, you're not dying in vain. Edna

Granger will get her retribution. A daughter's life for a daughter's life. She's willing to pay well for that revenge, enough to buy the drugs that may save my grandson's life."

Collette couldn't make sense of the man's mutterings. She closed her eyes and tried to block his voice from her mind, so that his face and voice would not be the last things she saw or heard.

Forcing the evil into the dark corners of her fading consciousness, she let Dylan's face play in her mind. She pictured him stepping onto the porch of the ranch house that very first day and the way he'd looked when he'd smiled and tipped his Stetson to the waiting reporters. Cocky, virile, rugged, handsome. A cowboy to build a dream on.

She should have told him that she loved him last night. Now it was too late.

Chapter Eighteen

Someone, probably the Hardware Stalker, had tampered with the elevators, leaving all of them stuck on the top floor. Dylan raced up the six flights of stairs, his endurance training paying off big-time.

He knew that Tommy Jo Benoit was in the hospital with his sights set on Collette, but Dylan's cell phone hadn't rung, which meant Collette was still with Eleanor. She was safe, he assured himself.

Adrenaline was still pumping through him like water rushing from a dam break when he reached the sixth floor. He scanned the hallway before he approached the guard.

"Is Collette McGuire still with the patient?"

"No. She left a few minutes ago."

Dylan checked his cell phone. No missed calls. No messages. "Where did she go?"

"I didn't ask. She didn't say, but she walked

off in that direction." The guard pointed toward the other end of the hall.

The assurances Dylan had fed himself on the staircase fell flat. He had to find Collette. She had to be okay. But why go off without calling him?"

A nurse's strident voice caught his attention. "I told you the bathroom in Room 614 needs cleaning. The patient vomited all over the floor."

Dylan turned to see a burly orderly defend himself.

"I lost my keys or someone took them," the man said. "I can't get to my supplies."

"Find someway to get to your mop bucket now," the nurse ordered.

Again Dylan felt his impending-danger signal vibrate through his body. He rushed to the orderly taking the verbal abuse. "Where do you keep your supplies?"

"In the closet down the hall. I had the keys hanging from my belt a few minutes ago, and now they're gone."

"Take me to the closet. And hurry."

The panic in his voice must have sounded convincing. The orderly started walking at a brisk pace.

"On the double," Dylan ordered in military fashion. "This could be life or death."

The orderly obeyed and started jogging down the hall.

"That's the closet," he said, "but I don't have the keys."

Dylan tried the door. It didn't budge, but he heard a scraping and bumping noise inside. "Open up," he ordered.

When no one did, he stood back and took a deep breath. "We have to break it down."

"No way, man. I'll end up having to pay for the repairs."

"Then get the hell out of the way."

Dylan threw his shoulder into the door, and the wood frame splintered. The orderly jumped into the act and on the second hit, the door came crashing down.

Dylan's worst nightmare faced him. Collette was scrunched into a corner, her eyes glazed over. Tommy Jo Benoit stood over her, the gun in his hand pointed at Collette's head.

The orderly backed away.

"Stay where you are," Benoit ordered.

Dylan sized up the situation. Collette's neck was red and her lips had a blue cast. Benoit had been choking her, killing her slowly, for his own pleasure. He was a trained assassin for the mob. Had he wanted, he could have broken her neck with one quick movement. Instead, he'd dragged it out, no doubt getting off on the sick pleasure of watching her die.

"Let Collette go," Dylan said. "This is Edna Granger's battle, not yours. If you kill Collette, you won't walk out of here alive. A paycheck isn't worth dying for."

"Sometimes it is. Say goodbye, Collette." Benoit poised to shoot.

Collette slumped into the corner. "I love you, Dylan. Please, don't be a hero. Not this time. Save yourself."

The words were so soft and hoarse that Dylan could barely make them out. He'd never set out to be a hero, but he could not let Collette die.

"You stinking, woman-killing coward," he spat. "They should have slit your throat instead of chopping off your tool."

Benoit shuddered in rage, and moved the gun so that it was pointed at Dylan's head. Dylan liked those odds a whole lot better.

That split second was all the opening he needed. He kicked the gun from Benoit's weakened hand, sending it clattering across the closet.

Brave now that Benoit was unarmed, the burly orderly tackled him to the floor while Dylan recovered the gun. He handed the weapon to the orderly. "If he makes one wrong move, shoot him."

Dylan fell to the floor beside Collette and

gathered her in his arms. He held her close while he called for help, his heart still beating erratically.

Had he been a few seconds later... Had he found Collette dead...

He couldn't bear the thoughts, so he held her close, thinking that he'd never let her go.

"And Dad said you were nothing but trouble," she murmured.

"Like I said before, your father is a very smart man."

Epilogue

Three months later

Eleanor lifted her glass of chardonnay as if she were toasting. "I love this garden."

"It was Helene's private oasis originally," Collette said. "I wanted to revive it as a tribute to her love for her family."

Melinda sat down on the ornate bench that had been spruced up with new paint. "Did you do all the work yourself?"

"No. Troy dug up the weeds and tilled the new beds. Dylan's been busy with repairs to the ranch, but he helped me mend the stone wall. I planted, watered and fertilized."

Eleanor did a pirouette, a bit awkwardly since she was wearing incredibly high heels with her belted pencil skirt. "I think this would be a beautiful spot for a wedding."

"You can borrow it anytime you want to tie the knot."

"I'm thinking of you and Dylan. You love him, so what's the holdup?"

"He's busy helping Troy get the ranch up and running."

Melinda looked perplexed. "So you're just going to keep living at the old Callister place indefinitely?"

"It's a nice house, and I have my photography business," Collette protested. "It's not as if I need a wedding ring to have a life."

She avoided the painful truth that although Dylan seemed as much in love with her as she was with him, he'd never once mentioned marriage.

Collette stooped to pull a new weed. "Aren't you two the same friends who were telling me how bad Dylan was for me just a few months ago?"

"We were wrong," Eleanor said. "We admit it. Which reminds me, what's the latest on your crazed stalker/assassin?"

"He's in jail awaiting trial. So is Edna Granger. When she started spilling her guts in hopes of a lesser charge, Benoit decided to follow suit. She hired him to kill me to get back at Dad for killing her daughter in the drug-induced domestic mayhem."

"I read about that," Melinda said, "but I still don't get the stalker routine."

"That was originally Edna's idea, but Benoit

elaborated on the scheme. They decided that if I told everyone I was being stalked before I was killed, that would mislead the investigators and keep them from suspecting that Edna or Benoit had a hand in my death."

"It might have worked if Dylan hadn't shown up in time that very first night." Eleanor said.

"Exactly." Collette swatted at a mosquito that had landed on her arm. "Benoit had knocked you unconscious and was waiting for me to arrive so that I could watch him kill you before he killed me. He has a taste for the macabre." She shuddered, despite the summer heat. "Good thing Dylan showed up and knocked a giant hole in his plans."

"So all's well that ends well?" Eleanor asked.

"At least it ended as well as could be hoped for Benoit's ill grandson," Collette said. "After his story received so much publicity, the insurance company decided to pay for the drug after all. He's in remission and back home with his parents in Marble Falls."

Both Eleanor and Melinda cheered that news.

"And how are things between you and your father?" Eleanor asked.

"Making progress."

"Great," Eleanor said. "He lacks tact when

questioning victims and he doesn't mince words, but I like the old buzzard."

"You would," Melinda said.

The talk turned from crime to the increasing sales of *Beyond the Grave* and their appreciation for Troy's letting them feature the house in the next edition. They'd taken dozens of pictures today.

An hour and a glass of wine later, they were ready to leave.

"I hate to lie to our readers," Melinda said as Collette walked them to Eleanor's car. "But this place is too peaceful to be haunted."

"Agreed," Eleanor added. "Too bad. If I were a ghost, I'd want to haunt a house just like this one."

If they only knew.

But they wouldn't hear it from Collette. It was a secret shared only by her and Helene.

DYLAN RODE UP on his recently purchased majestic black steed just as Collette was climbing into her Jeep. He looked every inch a cowboy, a deliciously intriguing cowboy.

"Leaving so soon?" he asked.

"I've been here all afternoon. Where were you?"

"I wanted to give you time with your friends. I didn't expect you to leave before I got back."

"A man should never keep a woman waiting indefinitely."

I'll try to remember that. Now that I'm here, why don't we take the horses for a ride and catch the sunset by the creek?"

The offer was too tempting to resist. "I guess I can stay awhile longer."

"I'll saddle Lady for you."

"Good. I'll get my boots from the trunk and meet you at the horse barn."

In minutes, they were galloping across the east pasture with endless stretches of hilly grassland stretching in front of them. She could have ridden like that forever, but when they reached the creek, Dylan slowed to a trot and then stopped beneath the sketchy shade of a lonesome pine tree.

A row of willow trees lined the creek bed. A blanket was spread out beneath them topped with a picnic basket and a cooler of champagne. She flushed with pleasure, then did her best to hide it.

Dylan helped her dismount and then took her hand and led her to the edge of the creek where the picnic was waiting.

For the first time since they'd met, he seemed awkward and a bit unsure of himself. Whatever he'd brought her here for, he obviously wasn't sure she'd like it.

Her heart plummeted. He was going to tell her that he'd done what he came to Mustang Run to do. He'd bonded with his father. He'd gotten the ranch up and running. It was time for him to move on.

He'd never promised her forever, but how would she ever live without him? She loved his voice, his humor, the way he swaggered, the way he made love with her. She loved him.

She wanted to lash out and beat her fists against his chest and beg him never to leave. That had never been her style. Instead she propped her hands on her hips. "Sure of yourself, aren't you, cowboy? Planning a picnic without asking first. I could have said no to your invitation for a ride."

"I'm glad you didn't. I wanted you to see this spot just before the sun dips below that strand of trees off to the west. It casts a magic glow over the area."

Dylan was all the magic she needed.

"I'm thinking of building a house here," he said. "What do you think?"

Her heart jumped to her throat. "Does that mean you're staying in Mustang Run?"

He took off his Stetson and tossed it onto the blanket. "All depends."

"On what?"

"The answer to my next question." He reached in his pocket and pulled out a gold band circling a solitary diamond. "I love you, Collette. I think of you all day when I'm working the ranch. Nights I don't see you, I go crazy with wanting you. For the first time in eighteen years, I feel like I'm where I belong. I'm thinking that means we should get married."

Her heart pounded. All she'd ever wanted from life was standing in front of her in the person of a heroic, protective, gorgeous cowboy. "Oh, Dylan. I love you, too. I have from the first moment we met."

"But do you love me enough to marry me? Think before you answer. Becoming a Ledger means being branded with that name and all the suspicions that go with it for the rest of your life. So will our children—unless you don't want children."

"Of course I want children, lots of them. Well, three, at least. And I'll make sure they are proud to be a Ledger, proud to be your sons or daughters."

"Is that a yes?"

"That, Dylan Ledger, is definitely a yes."

Dylan pulled her into his arms for a kiss that promised a lifetime of love.

Tears of happiness burned in Collette's eyes as

she thought of Helene and knew that somehow she was watching and that all heaven was cheering for the son of Troy Ledger who'd found his way home.

* * * * *

LARGER-PRINT BOOKS!

GET 2 FREE LARGER-PRINT NOVELS

PLUS 2 FREE GIFTS!

HARLEQUIN®

INTRIGUE®

Breathtaking Romantic Suspense

YES! Please send me 2 FREE LARGER-PRINT Harlequin Intrigue® novels and my 2 FREE gifts (gifts are worth about $10). After receiving them, if I don't wish to receive any more books, I can return the shipping statement marked "cancel." If I don't cancel, I will receive 6 brand-new novels every month and be billed just $4.99 per book in the U.S. or $5.74 per book in Canada. That's a saving of at least 13% off the cover price! It's quite a bargain! Shipping and handling is just 50¢ per book.* I understand that accepting the 2 free books and gifts places me under no obligation to buy anything. I can always return a shipment and cancel at any time. Even if I never buy another book from Harlequin, the two free books and gifts are mine to keep forever.

199/399 HDN E5MS

Name _____ (PLEASE PRINT) _____

Address _____ Apt. # _____

City _____ State/Prov. _____ Zip/Postal Code _____

Signature (if under 18, a parent or guardian must sign) _____

Mail to the **Harlequin Reader Service**:
IN U.S.A.: P.O. Box 1867, Buffalo, NY 14240-1867
IN CANADA: P.O. Box 609, Fort Erie, Ontario L2A 5X3

Not valid for current subscribers to Harlequin Intrigue Larger-Print books.

**Are you a subscriber to Harlequin Intrigue books and
want to receive the larger-print edition? Call 1-800-873-8635 today!**

* Terms and prices subject to change without notice. Prices do not include applicable taxes. N.Y. residents add applicable sales tax. Canadian residents will be charged applicable provincial taxes and GST. Offer not valid in Quebec. This offer is limited to one order per household. All orders subject to approval. Credit or debit balances in a customer's account(s) may be offset by any other outstanding balance owed by or to the customer. Please allow 4 to 6 weeks for delivery. Offer available while quantities last.

Your Privacy: Harlequin Books is committed to protecting your privacy. Our Privacy Policy is available online at www.eHarlequin.com or upon request from the Reader Service. From time to time we make our lists of customers available to reputable third parties who may have a product or service of interest to you. If you would prefer we not share your name and address, please check here. ☐

Help us get it right—We strive for accurate, respectful and relevant communications. To clarify or modify your communication preferences, visit us at www.ReaderService.com/consumerchoice.

HILP10R

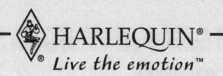

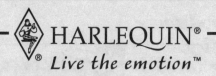

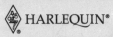

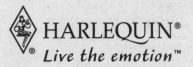